Special thanks to my early readers who encouraged me to finish this story, and especially to those who read it several times through all the edits! Notably: Penny Higgins, Stacy Valentine and especially Alice Miller, who gave me some useful insights for a 12 year old!

Also, to Max Lucado, who inspired me to write this whole story from an excerpt from his book, reprinted by permission, 'God Came Near,' by Max Lucado © 1986, Thomas Nelson Inc., Nashville, Tennessee. All rights reserved.

Cover artist: Grace Mills

Contact the author at: erasmusdrab@gmail.com for further insights and links about Drabacus.

CONTENTS

PROLOGUE

Hello Dear Reader,

I'm going to tell you a story that happened over a lifetime ago.

Many of the facts are true – but I can't tell you which ones.

I think by the end though you'll be able to work that out for yourselves.

1

A MYSTERY TO SOLVE

It's the summer of 1908, and the sea breeze is blowing gently on the shore of Marlinghampton, a popular holiday resort in the north of England.

An unexpected visitor has arrived looking for something to spoil. That's what He likes to do, and He doesn't care who He hurts in the process. Completely dressed in black, His long, dark, curly hair is blowing in the wind. He's a stranger to this town and He's going to make His mark.

'Oh yes', He thinks, looking at the beautiful fountain sat in the centre of the seaside town. As the high, shooting water cascaded down upon the chubby, naked figures in a ring he thought, 'I'll put a stop to that.'

So He did his deed and then sped off with the booty tucked under His arm. But – He was seen, oh yes, and she wasn't going to let Him get away with that!

Spin forward to 1972. It's the start of summer, and the Watson family are making their way to The Seafield Hotel in Marlingham, as it is now known. Mr Watson is in command of the driving and Mrs Watson is in charge of entertainment. On the back seat are best friends Susan and Pauline. Quite opposite in likes and dislikes. One an art-loving, dramatic brunette, the other, sporty, shy and blonde. Both however are moaning about the early start they had to make that morning.

Susan's baby brother John, now eight months old, and nicknamed 'Stinky' by her, is sleeping, blissfully unaware that boredom has firmly set in and is about to cause distraction.

'I wish we'd not had to set off sooo early,' moaned Susan, shifting her position again in frustration.

'I know,' yawned Pauline, 'we've missed 'Banana Splits'!' At once, the two friends burst into the opening title song of their favourite TV programme.

'Tra la la, tra lala la, tra la la, tra lala la, one banana, two bananas, three bananas, four…'

'Girls, do be quiet! You will distract your Father,' interrupted Susan's mother.

'Sorry Mum, but we're bored!' they chorused.

'Well, here you are then, I picked up your comics from the newsagent before we left. Pauline, your Mum has sent your 'Whizzer and Chips' too,' said Mrs Watson, handing out her trump cards.

'Oh Mum, you've rolled it up so tightly, you've creased all the free stickers. I can't wear any of them now!'

'Tuh, you just can't win,' said Mr Watson wearily.

'Not with teenage girls anyway,' chirped Mrs Watson. 'At least baby John is fast asleep for now.'

'We're not teenagers just yet,' announced Susan, as she settled down for a good read.

Pauline was accompanying Susan and her family for a visit to Mrs Watson's elderly mother. She had lived in Marlingham for most of her life, but had recently moved to an old people's home due to bad health, forcing the family to stay at one of the resorts' hotels, a new experience for all.

'Can I read your 'Whizzer and Chips' comic after you, Peewee?' inquired Susan, using her friend's nickname.

'If you consider changing to a Whizz Kid,' asserted Pauline with a smirk. This comic divided its readers into two gangs – Whizz Kids or Chipites. Susan and Pauline were on opposite sides.

'Hey, no way – Chipites rule! I'll buy my own before changing to a weak Whizz Kid!'

'Stop arguing you two, we are nearly there anyway, and be interested in your Grandma Susan. I think she's finding it hard to settle in the new home,' chirped Mrs Watson.

A half hour of peace reigned until Mr Watson suddenly announced, 'That's where we are staying.' All heads turned to look. The Seafield Hotel seemed to just grow out of the ground, forming a common bond with its surroundings, having a superior position on the rock head. As they passed by, having decided to call on Grandma first, they noticed some of the windows seemed to be buried right in the rock face and you could now see rusting metal steps unwinding from one of the rooms as an escape route to the sandy beach below.

'We'll go down those later,' commented Susan, ever the adventurer.

'Yeah, they could lead to smuggler's caves or anything,' Pauline replied excitedly.

'No,' retorted Susan, 'we're too far north for that, aren't we? I thought that only happened in Devon and Cornwall.'

'Well, who knows the secrets of Marlingham's beaches?' said Pauline in her best mysterious sounding voice.

Suddenly, diverting their attention on the other side of the road, came a noisy tram, one of Marlingham's old-fashioned features. 'Ooh,' commented Pauline, 'I'd like to ride one of those later.'

'Boring,' said Susan, having enjoyed many a ride over the twelve years of her life.

Pauline, who was new to the town, then caught sight of the most famous seaside attraction Marlingham had. Set high above the beach, it had been badly beaten with sea salt for over half a century. Clearly neglected, it hardly stood out. Five large cherubim statues, standing in a large ring looked all forlorn, their fruit bowls holding seemingly rotten fruit, as the green mould covered the once sparkling bronze. Below, its large dusty water basin was now filled with stray sand and last year's leaves. The surrounding weeds that had claimed the area were chocking five large water jets protruding from its centre. The feature being surrounded by a large, ornate and colourful garden area, making up for the faded spectacle.

'Ohh, look at that pond type thing,' said Pauline, unable to describe the dull attraction.

'It's actually a fountain, Peewee, but it's never worked for years,' Susan informed her.

'Has no-one thought of fixing it?' Pauline asked, puzzled that something once so lovely should remain out of action for so long.

'Don't think so,' replied Susan, returning to her comic, uninterested, due to the fact that she'd seen it every year.

The car journey over, they made their way to Mrs Fradds' new surroundings in the Duckshaw Manor rest home. 'Your room's much bigger than I expected Mother,' exclaimed Mrs Watson, after the initial kisses were over with.

'Yes,' Grandma Fradd nodded. 'I've been able to fetch most of my precious belongings with me.'

'In other words, your cupboards are full of rubbish Alice,' smiled Mr Watson.

'Alan, don't be so rude,' snapped Mrs Watson.

'He doesn't mean it,' said Susan, quick to his defence.

'You can help your dad make us all a nice cup of tea then, since you're so pally,' gestured Mrs Watson, pointing to the kitchen area in the corner of the room.

'Alan's right, Irene,' sighed Grandma, 'it's mostly rubbish I've brought.'

'How long's the fountain thingy not worked?' asked Pauline of Grandma, as she immediately noticed the picture of it in all its former glory on her wall.

'Oh yeah, she's not seen it before,' chirped Susan, from a steam-filled corner.

Mrs Fradds' well-lined face seemed to smooth out as she began to launch into an extended reply. Her soft face had natural, high-boned cheeks, bright red in colour, and her petite nose and lips gave her a childlike appearance in her old age. 'Let me tell you the story of how it came to be built,' she began, twisting into story mode position. 'Just before the turn of the century in 1897, the then Mayor of Marlinghampton, as the resort was officially known, Mr Francis Eaves, decided he wanted to celebrate entering into the twentieth century with a special commission for the town, which didn't really attract a lot of visitors, considering its seaside position. It was his thought that something spectacular, not seen on these shores before, may bring fame and distinction to the area, and draw people here for holidays to help expand the town's tourism industry. He sought one of France's most eminent architects, Monsieur Pierre Lavadan, who was world renowned for some of the most famous sites to be seen. In Paris, notably the Oblique a La Laroche,' said Grandma, using a French accent for effect.

'A magnificent fountain and garden area, which enticed vast crowds from all over the world, bringing prosperity to the city. After six months of persuasion, Monsieur Lavadan finally agreed, thinking it would increase his prominence as one of the world's leading designers. Work began on the fountain at the end of 1898, and it was finished on December 22nd 1899, just in time for the celebrations. By now, the earlier building work, which had taken over a year, had attracted many foreign newspapers. The opening ceremony, on Saturday 29th December, was one of the grandest affairs,' Grandma motioned, waving her hands up in a regal fashion.

'Attended by the Duke of Lancaster, many minor royals and most of the rich landowners of the region. Being French, Monsieur Lavadan created a most spectacular unveiling commemoration. When he switched on the water jets, the crowds gasped in awe at the splendid vision before them. The shimmering water spurting from the jets attracted the light like diamonds, cascading in arches, dancing down on the smooth, round shoulders of the proud cherubim, then, every so often, water would suddenly spurt from the ground in the surrounding garden areas, giving everyone a good wetting,' she laughed. 'My mother said it was breath-taking,' recalled Grandma, who had gestured the water falling, dramatically with her arms and hands.

'Monsieur Lavadan brought in the finest chefs from France to cater for all the important guests, serving the most wonderest meal in all of England that day.' Grandma was prone to making up the weirdest words to make it sound better. It was obvious from whom Susan had picked up her artistic talent, as she continued to act out her words. 'The whole weekend was noted as one of the most exquisite occasions to mark entering the twentieth century. It was decided a gala would be held each year to remember the jubilee event. Mayor Eaves had been quite correct in his prediction that it would bring glory and wealth to the town. In just five years, tourism in Marlinghampton had quadrupled. Many shopkeepers became rich and it was the place to be seen in, with many grand events.'

'So it was as popular as Blackpool or Brighton?' queried Pauline.

'More so!' Mrs Fradd replied, 'King Edward VII came to stay at The Seafield Hotel and the town was considered a 'Jewel in the North of England'.'

'Wow, I didn't know that!' said Pauline, amazed that the now quiet little town was such a famous place so long ago. 'So, what happened?' quizzed the ever curious Pauline on the end of her seat. Grandma took a deep breath, as in shock, and continued.

'Well, the fountain just stopped working. Funnily enough, it was about this time of year, back in 1908. No-one thought anything about it for a few days, thinking it was a problem with the pipes, but in a couple of weeks it was the talk of the town. The summer season was about to start and the visitors had already commented on how dull the garden area had become. The Mayor called an emergency meeting to investigate the matter. It was found by entering the fountain basement that the main key, which turned on the fountain spring, was missing!'

'Where was it?' asked Susan, suddenly becoming interested.

'It was nowhere to be found,' said Grandma, mysteriously.

'So why couldn't they make another?' interrupted Pauline.

'Aahh, that's because the key had a special numerical sequence on it, a particular trademark, which Monsieur Lavadan was known for. You had to insert the key in several different locks to unlock and release the intricate pumping device. They sought his advice, but upon enquiries to France, it was discovered that he had died two years earlier, in an outbreak of Scarlet Fever, that had killed many French citizens. No-one knew the complicated code, and to make matters worse, the plans of all his works were destroyed in a mysterious fire.'

'Ohhaa,' moaned Pauline, clearly getting involved in the story.

'Many folks tried to replicate it, a reward was offered to anyone who could crack the code, and there's a reward for the return of the key, which still stands today.'

'How much for?' asked Susan with great interest, as she passed piping hot tea to Grandma.

'Well, it was for five pounds, which was a lot of money then, equal to two month's wages!' exclaimed Grandma.

'Hmmm, it's still a summer's spends today,' said Pauline, winking at Susan excitedly.

'Alas,' Grandma continued sadly, 'six years later the war broke out and the matter became trivial compared to everything else, but the decline in tourism had begun already and things never really recovered,' sighed Grandma.

'And the culprit never came forward?' asked Susan.

'No, the Mayor was sure it was some joker who always intended to return it one day as a surprise, but they think they might have been killed in the war and the key lost forever,' replied Mrs Fradd, taking a well-earned sip of tea. 'And all that was sixty four years ago,' she sighed, exhausted and reminiscently saddened after her ten minute tale.

'How sad,' said Pauline, clearly dismayed at the story.

Everyone tucked into custard creams that Susan had found in Grandma's drawer.

'Don't scoff too many of those, Susan, you won't eat your lunch,' added Mr Watson, as he grabbed at least three. Everyone was feeling a bit peckish.

'You've grown quite big since I last saw you, Pauline,' remarked Mrs Fradd. 'Your hair is blonder and longer than ever! In fact, you're both growing up into very pretty young ladies.'

'Don't get them more big-headed than they already are,' said Mr Watson. 'Susan hogs our lounge mirror practically all day. Irene and I don't get a look in!'

Susan and Pauline were indeed quite pleasing to the eye but quite opposite in appearance. Susan's facial features were dark due to having a Great Grandpa from India, Mrs Fradds' father. She had deep set coal-coloured eyes underneath wild, bushy eyebrows and long, chestnut brown hair, which everyone always incorrectly described as black, always getting her mad, whilst Pauline was fair-skinned with bright blue eyes, being three inches taller and eight months younger. Both girls' complexions were soft and clear, the onset of spots some years away yet.

'What's the hotel like, mum?' enquired Mrs Watson.

Grandma turned to the girls to give her answer. 'It's fine love, and there's a nice surprise for you girlies,' teased the old lady. Eyes widened as Grandma blurted out the news. 'There's a real live monkey at The Seafield called Maddison.'

'No way,' replied the girls together.

'He does odd jobs around the hotel,' said Grandma, giving more intrigue.

'He seems very clever then,' exclaimed Pauline, now shifting her bum around on the chair with excitement.

'Don't forget to give him a tip,' suggested Grandma.

'That's a novel way of getting more money,' sneered Mr Watson. 'I suppose more people think it's cute giving money to a monkey.'

'Can we tip him, Dad?' inquired Susan, knowing full well he wouldn't.

'If you want me to give him some of your spending money I can,' said Mr Watson, knowing full well that her answer would be 'no'.

'If you gave me decent spends I could afford to give him a tip,' complained Susan loudly, but politely to her Dad.

'Same old row,' sang Mrs Watson, well used to the routine by now.

'I've not given you your holiday money yet,' interrupted Grandma, hoping to calm the situation. 'Here you are – a shiny fifty pence piece. You will share it with Pauline won't you?'

'Mother, that's very generous of you. Say thank you Susan.'

'Thank you Grandma!' said Susan, planting a big kiss on her Gran's cheek. 'I'll give Peewee half of it and we'll give

Maddison a little tip too,' raising her voice, fully intending her Dad to hear of her generosity.

After lots more chatter, the visit to Mrs Fradd ended and the family made their way to The Seafield Hotel to settle in before lunch.

2

WHO LOOKS LIKE FUN?

It was now in the full throws of rain, giving everyone a good wetting, as they ran awkwardly with their luggage towards the hotel entrance. The Seafield overlooked the clear, blue sea from the rear and was in an excellent vantage point off the corner of the main promenade, jutting out nicely to give a commanding view of the sandy beach from all sides. Mrs Watson's mother had recommended The Seafield as it was the closest to her new home.

The outside looked very grand but it needed re-painting. The once white walls had faded to a shade of grey, and its windowsills, beaten by sea salt, hardly had any paint on. But, for its faults on the outside, you could tell The Seafield, to most of its regular guests, was a home from home the minute you walked through the door. 'Wow,' said Susan, as the biggest fireplace she had ever seen, greeted her. 'Santa and all his reindeers could fit down that one!'

The hotel owner, Mrs Fishwick, had taken the liberty of lighting the now, glowing fire, due to the cold, dampening conditions. It did indeed welcome all the rain-spotted visitors entering the large, ornate reception area. Mrs Fishwick had a kindly face and two-tone hair, but looked as if she'd stand no nonsense. She welcomed the Watson family as if they were long-standing regulars. 'Sorry it's such a rotten day for your arrival!' she said, looking everyone up and down. 'But I've got a nice lunch to warm your tums – you'll want some hot milk too?' she enquired of Mrs Watson.

'Any minute now,' nodded Susan's Mum, as little John Peregrine stirred from another sleep. Mr Watson was very fond of Falcons and so had named his son after one of the birds, much to his mother-in-law's horror.

'My husband and his little friend will see to your cases, just leave them in the foyer – they'll be perfectly safe,' gestured Mrs Fishwick. 'Now, let me take you up to your rooms. I'm afraid the lift's not working today.'

The stairs began towards the back of the hotel, twisting around the main reception area three times. They were unusually wide, allowing four people to traipse the steps at the same time. The carpet was made up of rich red and black squares, which didn't quite meet the edges. Susan however, noticed something much more interesting that had begun to climb the many steps. 'He's here, Peewee,' squawked Susan excitedly. Pauline quickly peeped over the bannister and grinned from ear to ear.

'Ooh you've spotted Maddison by the sound of it,' smiled Mrs Fishwick to the two girls.

'Does he really live here?' inquired Susan excitedly.

'Is he house trained?' giggled Pauline.

'Oh yes,' replied Mrs Fishwick, confidently. 'He's a great attraction with all our guests.'

'He must be strong to lift the cases, but he doesn't look very big?' puzzled Pauline.

'He's stronger than Mr Fishwick,' she reassured the girls.

Maddison and Mr Fishwick had now caught up the intrigued party, since everyone had stopped on the staircase to gawp at the amusing sight. As the monkey approached, they could see his size and shape was that of a chimpanzee. But when he stood up tall, his head almost came up to Susan's chin and made her jump back in surprise. Sprouting from his head and face was a lion-type mane, two-tone grey in colour that matched Mrs Fishwick's, falling down beyond his shoulders. Maddison looked magnificent. The raven black hair, covering the rest of his body, with its touches of grey here and there, shone like silk. His black hands, each clutching a suitcase, were human-like in texture, the skin being smooth, as was his face. Well-padded out cheeks looked like they were hiding two gobstoppers either side. He was very handsome to look at, having a twinkle in his soft, green eyes, and a knowing smile across his gentle face. He wore a simple bright blue felt waistcoat, with a small red pouch around his hips, which Mr Fishwick said, was for tips. The words, 'The Seafield Hotel', had been neatly sewn onto the front, confirming Maddison's place in the world.

'Give him a stroke, love,' said Mr Fishwick. 'He won't bite you.'

'How old is he?' asked Susan, as she stretched out her hand cautiously to do so.

'Well, he's lived here thirty years with us, and he belonged to the previous owners before that. We aren't too sure of how old he is, but he never seems to get any older to us,' came back the long, but unanswered reply by Mrs Fishwick.

'I think he's wonderful, we must take some pictures of him,' Susan begged her Mum.

'Of course, but let's get unpacked, we've got all week,' said Mrs Watson, laughing.

Susan and Pauline shared a room, which disappointingly was at the front of the hotel, overlooking the wide, sand-filled promenade. Mr and Mrs Watson had paid the extra to have the breath-taking view of the ocean, which constantly beat against the rocks below the hotel kitchens. The girls' room was narrow, with a pink candlewick-covered bed either side of the salt speckled window. The deep piled pink and peach carpet was like a sponge to walk on and tickled their toes, as they kicked off their shoes in an attempt to make themselves at home in the unfamiliar surroundings. On plain white walls hung two uninteresting pictures of country cottages, in thick white wooden frames, which somehow didn't fit into a room by the sea.

There was the slight smell of salt and fish under the sash window, as if someone had left it open on a really blustery, rainy day. The room faced east, and the sun was just leaving the left hand corner of the bed Susan had chosen, and would not be seen again until the next morning.

'Hey, where's the red plastic bag P?'

'Thought you were bringing that in?' replied Pauline.

'It's got all tonight's chocolate ration in!' cried Susan. 'Have you left it in the car?'

'Must have. Sorry. We can get it later, can't we?'

'Not without my Dad noticing it, I was hoping to smuggle it in with everything else,' moaned Susan, who always had everything planned, whereas Pauline tended to go with the flow.

Quickly changing the subject, Pauline chattered away. 'Fancy having a real monkey in the same hotel. Carol, Michelle and Kay will be sooo jealous when they see the pictures.' She smirked as she put away her clothes.

'That's why we've got to take some, they'll never believe us otherwise,' retorted Susan, who was always telling tales and prone to exaggeration.

'Shall we go and look for him now?' asked Pauline excitedly.

'Hey, he might sit with us in the dining room,' replied Susan. 'I'm starving. I hope it's something good for lunch,' she said, the hunger overtaking her curiosity of the monkey. 'Let's go.'

Maddison was nowhere to be seen in the mint-green dining room, and the smell of fresh, hot, sea-fish pie, distracted everyone's enquiries of him until it was fully rested at the bottom of the girl's bellies. Susan was informed that Maddison was taking his regular afternoon nap. As the family collected their things to leave the dining room, a rather noisy family were entering.

The culprits, were two boys, arguing intensely, deaf to the cries of their parents, and completely unaware of the disturbance it was causing. The girls caught first sight of Mrs Fishwick looking vexed. She liked to run a nice, quiet and refined hotel, this spectacle portraying the opposite, with both boys almost coming to blows. Mrs Watson ushered out her party, politely ignoring the boy's parent's troubles.

'I bet they're brothers,' said Susan. 'They just remind me of my cousins, Tony and Graham, they never stop fighting. My poor Auntie Freda is always shouting at them.'

'Right girls,' commanded Mrs Watson. 'We'll go shopping this afternoon. Take no longer than ten minutes to get ready, and we'll meet you in the reception area. Don't forget your key either!' she smiled.

Susan and Pauline were ready in three minutes flat, both having decided to wear their fairly new blue 'Brutus' flared jeans and simple white T-shirts. The rain had now stopped and it felt quite warm. As the girls approached the reception area, they couldn't help but make their journey extra slow as they passed the dining room. The noisy family had completely forgotten their troubles as they too enjoyed the delicious fare on offer that lunchtime.

The older boy had dark brown hair, like Susan's, which draped just below his ears. A middle parting sat above his well-stocked eyebrows. His brother, in contrast, had ash-blonde hair, cut short, probably by his mum, due to the wide fringe above his left eye being a little crooked. Both boys donned bottle-green jumpers with V-necks.

'Do you think they'd be any fun?' queried Pauline.

'I dunno,' said Susan slowly. 'They're certainly quite lively, we do know that!' she continued cautiously, getting a good eyeful of the older boy. 'They could be a big pile of trouble!'

'Oh S,' sighed Pauline, abbreviating Susan's name as she often did, 'you never think anybody's OK. I bet they're really good fun when you get to know them,' Pauline said confidently.

'Hmmmm,' nodded Susan, 'he's quite nice looking,' she said, smiling, referring to the older brother.

'Yes,' agreed Pauline, quickly staking a claim. 'The younger one is quite cute too.' All debate came to an end as Mr and Mrs Watson appeared at the desk to give in room keys.

'Have you given yours in?' questioned Mr Watson, eager to get going. He quite liked shopping.

'No – here it is,' said Susan in a flash, throwing it underarm, rounder's fashion at her Dad. 'Good catch Dad!'

3

THOSE NOISY BOYS!

Arriving back with two bags on each arm, the mission was accomplished as Pauline managed to smuggle in the red tuck bag along with all the day's shopping. The girls were eager to try on their new clothes.

'The lift's working now,' said Pauline, as she entered the reception area. 'I've just seen the doors closing.'

'Oh good,' said Mrs Watson. 'These bags are heavy.'

'Actually Irene, I fancy a drink before dinner, are you coming to the bar?' said Mr Watson, heading that way already.

'Oh yes, good idea, you girls go up to your room and start getting ready, we'll meet you in the dining room in twenty five minutes,' said Mrs Watson, as she turned baby John's pram towards the bar. The little fella was out for the count.

Susan and Pauline entered the lift, meeting their own reflections. The whole lift was covered in mirrors on its three walls, with an ornate, green glass lampshade sticking out high on one side.

'Ooh, I like this lift Peewee,' said Susan, adjusting her fringe to the left.

'So do I,' added Pauline, pushing back her shoulders. 'It's not often you see a full-length view of yourself – I wish I didn't slouch so much.'

The lift reached the fourth floor. Both girls skipped along the corridor and entered their tiny room. As they started to discuss what they had bought that day, Pauline noticed the noisy boys and their parents returning from a walk along the promenade.

'Those boys looked bored stiff,' she remarked.

'Let's have a look,' said Susan, dashing over to the window. 'Tee hee, I bet they're never allowed out on their own,' giggled Susan.

'I hope their room isn't near ours, I'm not putting up with all their noise all night,' said Pauline, fishing at the back of one of the rickety drawers for an un-crumpled jumper.

'Oh, I hope it is, we can play knock and run. Hey, let's see which room they go into,' gestured Susan, leaping to the door. Both girls crept about the fourth floor, their ears straining to hear the slightest clue as to which rooms the family were staying in.

'Suppose they've gone for a drink like your Mum and Dad,' whispered Pauline, as they wandered about the quiet corridor.

'Well, even if they have, the boys won't be allowed in the bar,' Susan whispered back, as she silently approached the head of the stairs.

There was definitely some commotion below. The girls peered over the large, ornate bannister to the lower floor. The older boy was encouraging his younger brother, who looked no older than nine, to walk along the narrow bannister rail. It looked dangerous, and both girls became concerned for the young boy's safety. Dashing down the steps, Susan and Pauline began to intervene. 'Hey you, that's extremely dangerous. Help him down NOW!' Susan commanded.

The older boy, startled at who was giving such an order, looked directly at both girls with a scowl on his face.

'Just keep your nose out, sissy girls, my brother's an expert gymnast!' he said, defiantly.

'Suppose he falls? He'll be an expert at eating hospital food then,' replied Susan with gusto.

'That's if he's not killed first,' interrupted Pauline.

'Let him do some balancing on something low down, not three floors up,' said Susan, wisely.

'I am rather frightened Dean,' said young Michael, his knees beginning to shake on the bannister.

'Don't be a sissy too, you can easily walk that,' Dean egged him on.

'You do it then,' dared Susan, quickly trying to spare the young boy embarrassment.

'Easy,' he replied. Dean helped Michael down off the rail, then confidently leaped up with the ease of a tiger. Crouching low to the rail, he slowly began to straighten up.

Both girls' hearts were racing. They hadn't expected him to do it. It was very foolish, but he did seem to make it look very easy as he began to balance finely and walk towards them.

'See! – Wanna try it?' said Dean, triumphantly.

'No, can you get down please,' Susan said, feeling guilty at challenging him to do something so stupid.

The three with their feet firmly on the ground couldn't help admiring Dean's circus act, although the girls didn't let on. Feeling embarrassed, the girls turned around and headed back upstairs to their room. Dean was quite annoyed that his new audience was leaving so soon, he had wanted to show off a few tricks, and momentarily lost concentration. Suddenly, his foothold slipped. Scraping his shoe against the polished rail edge, his balance began to topple on the side that dropped three floors.

The girls looked down, alerted by a loud shout of 'Arrrgh', just in time to see Dean leaping towards the downward slope of the rail in an effort to save himself from the huge fall, and straddling it like a horse in mid gallop. Unfortunately for Dean, because of its downward direction, he began to fly down backwards by the seat of his pants, comic book fashion, his feet continuously banging against the side spindles competing with his screams, making rather a lot of noise. Susan and Pauline were filled with dread and delight at the same time, as they enjoyed the very entertaining, and unplanned performance. Noticing Dean seemed to survive hitting the floor with a bump, Susan shouted down to him.

'That's one way to get down – but try the lift next time, it's much safer!' Both girls smirked their 'told you so' expressions, hurting Dean all the more.

'That'll teach him to act so clever,' said Susan, smugly.

Just then, another treat appeared before them. Mrs Fishwick had heard all the noise, and had hurried to the scene, catching Dean rubbing his sore behind. Guessing he'd been sliding down the bannister, albeit involuntarily, she began to scold him loudly. A crowd soon gathered, amongst them Dean's father, looking very cross and embarrassed. After a ticking-off, greatly enjoyed by Susan and Pauline, Dean was ordered to his room with the promise of no tea.

'That reminds me, I'm starving!' said Susan, as they began on back to their room, the show finally over.

'Oh, I feel sorry for him now,' said Pauline, sorrowfully.

'I suppose I do really, it was us that made him do it,' agreed Susan with a sorrowful smile. 'I know, maybe we can find out what room he's in and leave him something outside his door?'

'Good idea S,' nodded Pauline, as they ran back to their room, feeling less guilty.

Twenty minutes had passed since Mrs Watson had instructed them to be ready, and they hadn't even got changed yet.

The dining room was full of hungry holiday makers. Thankfully, Mrs Watson had remembered to reserve their table. Others would have to wait until 8.30pm.

'No sign of Dean, Peewee,' said Susan, carefully scanning all the many different faces at tables of four and six. All of a sudden, Michael appeared with his Mum and Dad at the dining room door. They were seated two tables away. The two girls eagerly watched the family throughout the meal of roast beef and Yorkshire puddings. 'Well, they've not saved anything for Dean,' observed Susan, under her breath.

'Gosh, I couldn't go without my tea,' said Pauline, equally as quiet. 'What have you got left?'

'I've saved a boiled potato, one roast potato and a tiny slice of my beef. But how are we going to get it to our room?' Susan asked, originally thinking it would have been ok in a napkin.

'Be prepared! As the Brownie motto says,' declared Pauline, as she began to finish drinking her orange juice.

'Aha, your Tupperware mug! Blimey P, I wondered why you'd brought it down from the room. I'm impressed.'

'With my lump of cabbage, slice of beef and your stuff, he'll have a bit to tuck into, provided he doesn't mind it all mashed up together!' said Pauline, pleased that she had impressed Susan with her genius.

'He ain't getting any of the chocolate cake though, hey hey.'

After the sweet was eaten, the girls made an excuse to leave the table on urgent business, and left like a couple of spies about to complete an important mission. 'Right,' announced Pauline, just outside the lift. 'We just need to find out which room he's in now,' she said, pressing the button to call the lift.

'Ah well, that's been sorted,' Susan said smugly, at her bit of forward thinking. 'I asked at Reception when you went to the loo before dinner. It's Room 204 on the second floor.'

'Ye-e-es,' chanted both girls, as they slapped their hands together in contentment at everything coming together so easily.

As the lift doors opened, there was Maddison by himself. 'Aahh, hi Maddison,' cried the girls gleefully. They began stroking him at once. His soft green eyes seemed to smile, and his cute black nose twitched, as he smelt the food in Pauline's mug.

'Oh sorry Maddy, this is for someone who's not having any tea tonight because he's been naughty,' explained Susan, as if he would understand. 'I'll tell you what you can have though,' she said thoughtfully. Reaching down into her pocket, she found a shiny two pence piece, which she held to Maddison's eyes. 'Here you are little monkey, I promised my Grandma I'd give you some spends,' dropping it into his small red pouch. A tiny chink was heard, as it joined many half and one penny coins that had been received that day. Maddison seemed to nod in approval, a trick he'd obviously been taught as a response to people tipping him. After five minutes of fussing and patting Maddison, the girls finally found Room 204. They gave a quiet knock after they'd rehearsed what they were going to say to him, constantly looking left and right in case his parents came back.

'Are you sure it's this room?' asked Pauline anxiously, after there was no immediate reply.

'Quite sure,' Susan assured her, giving a louder knock this time. The trio of bangs to the door seemed to echo throughout the whole of the second floor. Pauline's forehead began to moisten as she began sweating, as she often did in tense situations. Suddenly, the unexpected happened.

'Hey, you two!' shouted a voice from around the L-shaped corridor. Both girls nearly jumped out of their skins. Seeing Dean outside the room had startled them.

'O, there you are!' exclaimed Susan, rather embarrassed at being caught unaware. 'We thought you might like a bit of food?'

'Yeah, we heard you had to miss tea,' said Pauline, shyly. 'Sorry it's cold.'

'And here's a chocolate bar, a little melted, but better than nothing I suppose,' added Susan.

'Thanks,' said Dean, immediately diving into the chocolate bar. 'I'm starved! I sneaked out to see if I could find anything, but no luck.' The next fifteen minutes were spent laughing at that afternoon's caper on the stairs, and a firm friendship was formed with introductions and details swapped with interest.

'We're here for the week,' announced Dean finally. 'Fancy doing some exploring?'

'Definitely,' they eagerly replied. 'See you tomorrow after breakfast.'

Susan and Pauline hurried back to their room, having discovered that it was two floors directly above the brothers. It was now getting late. The sun had set ten minutes earlier, leaving a red-orange glow to the sky.

'Red sky at night, shepherd's delight,' quoted Susan, gleefully.

'Let's hope so,' said Pauline. 'I'm dying to get down on the beach and into those caves. Who knows what we may find?'

Mrs Watson came to say it was bedtime and they could read until ten o'clock, but expected lights out promptly after that.

'Got tonight's chocolate ration Peewee?'

'Sure have – one Twix and one Walnut Whip each,' she replied, licking her lips in anticipation of the pleasure to come.

'Yum, whose allocation did Dean's chocolate come out of?' queried Pauline.

'Baby John's, of course!' giggled Susan, as she fumbled for her pyjamas.

The beds were cold to the touch and made each girl shiver as they each made an attempt to make a snug place to sleep. 'It's been a long day,' yawned Pauline.

'I know, we seem to have done so much! We've met the monkey...'

'Oh, he's so cute,' interrupted Pauline.

'As I was saying...'said Susan, irritated and obviously tired after a day of new experiences. 'We've met Maddison, had a laugh with Dean and we can look for that missing fountain key for something to do this week,' she added with a yawn.

'I don't think we'll find it,' said Pauline, rather pessimistically.

'Typical Peewee comment!' retorted Susan. 'Giving up before you've even had fun trying – just think if we got that five pounds reward!'

'Oh, I know, I've already worked out we could buy 125 Walnut Whips or 166 Twix bars,' Pauline informed her, Maths being one of her top subjects at school.

'Heaven,' Susan cried. 'We'll go for the Twix's, that's five and a half month's supply as opposed to only four month's Walnut Whips, plus we always leave the walnuts on top. What a waste that would be!'

'We could feed them to the birds in winter,' said Pauline thoughtfully, licking the cream out of her Walnut Whip.

'No, we'll sell them to my Dad for half a pence each. He loves them. We'd be able to buy another 15 then,' Susan quickly worked out.

'Then sell him the walnuts off the top of those and that's another seven pence, which will just buy one Walnut Whip and one Twix,' added Pauline, 'leaving a half pence spare.'

'Why half a pence?' queried Susan, who then quickly realised it would come from the final nut sold to her Dad. 'No, the Twix's will last longer as there's two bars in each,' Susan decided finally, picking hers up to munch.

'Y' know,' announced Pauline, 'I bet no-one's thought of looking in those caves for that key.'

'Course they will have,' exclaimed Susan. 'The reward would have bought about 3000 Twix bars back then in 1908, everyone would have been looking for it.'

'Aahh yes, but someone stole it, so I think people thought to look for it in someone's house, not the beach,' argued Pauline.

'Hmmm, maybe,' Susan answered, running it through her mind.

'I wonder why it was stolen?' asked Pauline, 'whoever did it was really mean.'

'Hmmm, proper mean,' muttered Susan, her brain quite tired after all the day's events and mental arithmetic regarding chocolate bars.

Pauline, also with heavy eyelids, just managed to screw up her chocolate wrapper, remembering that neither of them had cleaned their teeth, before she fell asleep.

As Mrs Watson popped her head quietly around the door about eleven o'clock, she was met with clothes dropped where they had been taken off, and chocolate wrappers between the beds on the floor. Turning off the little lamp, which had been a source of comfort, she commented to Mr Watson, 'they've made the place like home already!'

4

A FRIENDSHIP FORMED

Day two of the holiday started with a peep of sunlight catching Pauline's pillow. It was already well past eight thirty, and many guests had been down for breakfast. Mrs Watson cheerily entering the room, disturbed a peaceful sleep. 'Come on girls, rise and shine to a lovely sunny day,' she announced. Susan stirred, the thought of the day's adventures calling. Suddenly, she sprang out of bed, flabbergasting her Mum in the process. With a big stretch, followed by a shiver, she answered her Mum.

'Thanks Mum, we are awake see, up and out of bed and ready for breakfast.'

'You'll be lucky, it takes you an age to get ready and they stop serving at nine,' retorted Mrs Watson.

Pauline had now prised one eye open. The thought of no food horrified her. As Mrs Watson left the chilly, sunlit room, Susan announced that they'd better put 'Plan B' into action. Pauline agreed, and both girls were dressed in under ten minutes. 'Plan A' was to get washed, dressed, then breakfast. 'Plan B' was get dressed, get breakfast, get washed!

Sporting crumpled blue jeans, T-shirts and uncombed hair, both girls ran down to the busy dining room to join the rest of the Watsons, already tucking into bacon and eggs. A delightful smell when you are hungry. After a comment from Mr Watson, something about being likened to tramps, the girls spotted Dean and Michael by the window. They had almost finished, Dean having made up for missing his meal last night by almost eating a full loaf of toast.

'We've made some new friends already,' Susan informed her Mum and Dad confidently.

'Oh, who'd have you as friends?' joked Mr Watson, 'especially looking like you do this morning!'

'Dad, I've told you, we're getting washed and stuff later.'

'I do hope so love,' added Mrs Watson, 'you both look like well-fed workhouse girls.'

'And when you say washed…,' queried Mr Watson, 'do you mean a proper shower or your usual cat lick in the sink?'

'I've never smelt. I've checked with Mum,' uttered Susan, matter of factly, undaunted by her Dad's teasing. Dean and Michael began to get up from their table, followed by their Mum and Dad.

'Hi,' said Dean, as he passed by the table, 'what are you up to today?'

'Mum, Dad, this is Dean, his brother Michael, and his parents, Mr and Mrs Chapman. They come from Hurst Brook. That's not too far from where Auntie Mags lives is it?' introduced Susan with a smile. As the adults made their acquaintance, the four youngsters made arrangements to meet in Reception at 10am.

Back in their room, the girls began to get dressed into clean, ironed clothes. 'That shower's really refreshing,' said Pauline. 'Pity it's so far away down the hall.'

'I know,' said Susan, her cheek pressed against the window pane. 'You can just about see the beach and half that big rock face if you look from here.'

'Wouldn't it be better to open the window S?'

'I tried when you were having your shower, but it's stuck and feels like it will drop out if you pull too hard,' replied Susan, quite frustrated.

'You can just about see the fountain thingy the other way,' observed Pauline.

'Hey, do you think Dean and Michael will want to look for the key?' asked Susan.

'We'd have to split the reward money,' replied Pauline quickly.

'It's still 83 Twix's,' cried Susan, 'and anyway, you said we'd have no chance of finding it last night.'

'Well, it'll be fun trying like you said,' acknowledged Pauline, tying the laces of her white pumps. 'It's good that the lads like gymnastics like us. I wonder how many badges they have?' queried Pauline, ever competitive.

'Did Michael say he was eight or nine?' muffled Susan, cleaning her teeth.

'Nine, and Dean's just turned fourteen last week,' replied Pauline, as she shoved last night's sweet wrappers under the bed.

'Ready for off then?' said Susan, pleased at the big improvement in her appearance.

'Oh, that's much better,' cried Mrs Watson, as the girls popped in to say they'd see them at dinnertime.

It was quicker to go down the stairs than catch the lift. From the staircase windows they noticed a big, black cloud looming over the sea, and definitely heading towards Marlingham. 'Aww typical, look how dark it's getting now! That's the beach out for this morning,' Susan exclaimed.

'BOO,' shouted Dean and Michael together.

'Eeek!' was the loud response from the surprised girls.

'We heard you coming, so we thought we'd frighten you,' laughed Dean, as they both stepped from round the corner.

'You made me jump,' said Pauline, her heart still racing.

The four made their way down to the ground floor, discussing the oncoming cloud and its implications. Michael had also brought his new tape recorder along, one of the latest tiny portable models. The pals discovered that they all enjoyed the same cartoon characters, Catch the Pigeon, Wacky Races, Magpie, and of course, Banana Splits, whose theme tunes had all been recorded off the telly by Michael. They all sang together, each secretly competing to sound the best, but not one of them was gifted in this area.

'Let's explore the hotel,' suggested Michael shyly, switching off his tape player to save the batteries.

'Yep, there's a whole wing that's not been used for thirty years,' added Dean excitedly. Michael's face lit up, pleased at his big brother's agreement. It wasn't often Dean wanted to do what he suggested. Dean and Michael got on quite well for brothers, believe it or not, often dressing in the same clothes as they had today, navy blue collared T-shirts and white shorts.

'How do you get to it?' asked Susan.

'Will it be safe, if it's so old?' queried Pauline, ever so cautious.

'Course it will,' Dean claimed confidently.

How do you get to it?' repeated Susan, impatiently.

'We'd not have to be seen,' cautioned Dean, 'but next to the lift are the doors to the kitchen. You've to nip through them quickly, then up the first flight of stairs.'

'How do you know all this?' asked Pauline, growing more nervous by the minute at the thought of getting caught by Mrs Fishwick.

'Dean and I found it on our last afternoon here this Easter,' answered Michael, proud of their discovery.

'Yeah, we've been dying to explore since then,' Dean explained. 'Especially when we saw Maddison the monkey going that way.'

'How do you know he went up and not through the kitchens?' Susan queried.

'Cos we peeped, and saw his furry foot just disappearing around the corner at the top of the stairs,' said Dean.

'Ooh, he might live up there then, eh?' said Pauline to Susan.

'Right, I'm in,' nodded Susan, with Pauline quickly agreeing, excitedly.

As they reached Reception, Dean took command. 'It's going to be hard getting through those doors. Let's just watch for a while and see how often anybody goes in and out,' Dean instructed, like an army Captain on a recapture exercise. He was used to taking the lead. He captained the gymnastics and football teams at school; usually played the lead role in any play, and his scoutmaster had allowed him to command a team of cubs on an overnight stop-out, such was his trust in him. He didn't ever brag about these things though, his kid brother would do all that.

It was hard keeping watch and not looking suspicious at the same time. The hotel receptionist kept looking over, right into Pauline's eye, and she began to feel guilty. 'I'm sure he knows what we're up to,' Pauline whispered. 'He keeps looking right at me!'

'Peewee, it's just your imagination. He's no idea,' replied Susan calmly, confident that he wasn't a mind reader. Dean, overhearing Pauline's concern, gave a fresh instruction.

'Michael and I will go to the stairs and watch from there, you two sit by the fireplace, listening to the music as a distraction, and pretend you're waiting for someone. Michael and I will not be as noticeable then.'

'OK, I've made it one person going through every thirty seconds or so up to now,' Susan reported.

As the boys left to take up their fresh positions, Susan smiled at the receptionist. He did seem to be watching them! Thankfully, a couple of families arrived to distract him fully for a period of about fifteen minutes. The girls were able to confirm that the doorway was indeed a busy one. Getting bored, they made their way to join the brothers on the stairs. They all agreed that the door was probably going to be busy until the middle of the afternoon, when lunchtime was over and there might be a bit of a lull. Pauline secretly felt relief at the delay.

'So, it's two hours to dinner, any suggestions?' said Dean, hopeful of an exciting alternative. Susan looked at Pauline with raised eyebrows.

5

THE TEST

'Do you want to go and see a fountain?' she offered.

'A fountain!' moaned the boys at the seemingly boring proposal.

The girls quickly raised the point that there could be money to be made, and began to explain the story told by Grandma Fradd. Dean and Michael were soon enthused by Susan's story- telling and agreed it would be worth the investigation; well there was nothing else to do.

The fountain was only seven minutes away on foot. It made a nice little walk, despite the small spots of rain now and again. As the new-found pals trotted along, the fresh sea breeze made them feel alive and cheerful. Along the way, more tales were swapped, and a display of gymnastic talents was promised for later on that day.

'It's a mucky old thing,' observed Dean, looking into the large basin which had brown watermarks, suggesting some muddy person had bathed in it and not cleaned it out afterwards.

'You'd be a bit dirty if you'd not washed for sixty four years,' quipped Pauline.

'It's a shame really,' commented Susan, as she stepped over the rail for a closer look. 'IF it was cleaned up, it would be really pretty again.'

'They've not bothered with it, have they?' said Dean, noticing a square, bronze plate lid to the left of the fountain basin. Attached to it was an ornate handle, which could hardly be seen due to years of ingrained dirt and muddy sand which surrounded it. Weeds had grown all around, hiding it and sealing the edges. It hadn't been opened for over half a century.

'Do you reckon that leads down to the pump house?' Dean inquired as he stamped on it, loudly creating a hollow sound, giving away the fact that something interesting lay below. The others joined him. 'So your Grandma says the key was stolen from here?' Dean strained to ask, as he feebly attempted to prise the handle from its resting place. The ground wouldn't unlock its secret. 'It's just not budging!' Dean exclaimed.

'I've got my pen knife,' offered Michael.

'Everything seems to be sealed,' added Susan, as she too struggled to make any movement to the years of soil firmly embedding the lid to the ground.

'It's probably dangerous down there anyway,' suggested Pauline, getting anxious. Some passers-by had noticed the quartet acting suspiciously and she was afraid they would call the Police.

'Come on, let's leave it for now,' said Dean, feeling beaten, his efforts at moving the lid futile. 'You'd need a crow bar and a long dark night to have any chance of a peep down there with all these nosy parkers!'

'Just because we can't get in, doesn't mean we can't hunt for the key though,' said Susan, trying to keep the enthusiasm going.

'It would have been brilliant if we could have gone down the hole,' said Michael, bustling with the thought of an adventure. The four exchanged further views about the layout of the fountain, working out that the passageways to the pump must be twenty feet long. They would have to go back in the dark, but first they needed to figure out how to lift the lid.

'You know,' exclaimed Susan suddenly, 'I bet someone in this town knows something about it, after all, the thief must have bragged about it, they always do!'

'What, and some distant relative may have some clues?' asked Dean casually, tossing a pebble along the pathway.

'But how do we find out who they are?' Pauline asked glumly, now feeling the whole task was just impossible.

'We could put up a board by the fountain or at the front of the hotel, asking for information,' Susan announced, sure that it would bring some kind of response.

'The papers might pick up the story,' suggested Dean.

'Let's explore the caves on the beach first,' said Pauline, worried that too much attention would activate lots of bored holidaymakers, who might just claim the reward. 'I've a really good feeling the caves are a sure bet for a hiding place.'

'When's dinner?' Michael asked after his tummy stopped gurgling. The others laughed at his basic mind-set and they started back to The Seafield.

The mystery had entertained the foursome, passing the whole morning off. Lunch passed off another hour and ten minutes, and it was soon time to go back on patrol. Now two o'clock, the staff had almost finished clearing away the lunch plates, cups and cutlery, the pots clattering endlessly as they were piled onto trolleys that squeaked like a thousand budgies, as they were wheeled back to the kitchen.

Meeting at the bottom of the staircase, the four would-be explorers decided to wait until the afternoon receptionist came on duty. Using her, 'I'm interested in your job' routine, Susan found out that he changed with someone else at three o'clock.

Having a whole hour to kill, they decided to take a look outside. The rain had now stopped drizzling, and the children's play area looked promising. Michael was especially pleased. Being three years younger than the girls, he headed straight for one of three empty swings. Around twenty children were staying at the hotel that week. The sound of laughter, squeals and shouts of joy filled the air. It was all a bit noisy for Susan and Pauline, but then to their delight, they spotted a low balancing beam in the corner. 'Come on Peewee, before anyone else gets it!' Susan uttered, as she quickened her pace to secure first go. 'I wish I'd brought my leotard,' she said, jumping on gracefully but then wobbling in her haste. Pauline followed behind.

While the girls settled into their well-rehearsed routines, Dean got lumbered with the task of pushing Michael on the swing. To make it more entertaining for himself he began to push rather hard.

'Do you want to go as high as a kite Michael?' shouted Dean. Michael's wails of 'that's enough' fell on deaf ears as Dean tested out his strength. Michael's bottom left the seat of the swing, his hands losing grip on the rusting chain. Suddenly the momentum of the swing went hiddly piddly, and Dean was unprepared for Michael's body, now hanging a foot lower than the seat. As it came hurtling back to the ground, Michael's feet propelled into Dean's chest as he came forward to stop his brother. Both boys ended up in a heap, thankfully on the grass.

'Yet another fine display,' giggled Susan, drawn into the excitement by all the noise.

'Dean will seriously hurt his brother one day, he takes too many risks,' added Pauline in a much more serious mode. Susan dismounted.

'Let's go and see if they are alright,' she said, skipping to the spectacle, which had turned many small heads at play.

'What's this?' asked Pauline, stopping in her tracks. As she bent down she could see it was a small, red pouch, rather like the one worn by Maddison.

'It's Maddison's for definite,' Susan said knowingly. Dean and Michael hobbled over, each confirming that it did indeed belong to the monkey.

'He must play here,' said Dean. 'What's inside?' he asked.

'Several coins and sweets,' Susan replied as she further unfastened the pouch.

'What kind of sweets?' asked Michael, his mouth watering.

'Sugar bonbons, hmm, my favourite,' she said. Peeping further, Pauline cried, 'There's about 64, 67, 70 pence in here!' and began to count it out onto her hand.

'That's 23 Twix bars or 17 Walnut Whips,' Susan calculated quickly. Michael stretched out his hand to grab a bonbon.

'No,' shouted Dean, surprising the girls with his honesty. They agreed wholeheartedly with his decision. They couldn't eat Maddison's toffees.

'He'll love his sweets Michael, they are a real treat for him. It wouldn't be right to take them,' he explained.

'Ok, it's tempting I know, but we need to return this to Reception,' suggested Susan quickly, before she changed her mind.

'I agree,' added Dean. 'Let's return it right now, besides I've loads of holiday money,' he bragged. Pauline, in full agreement with Dean and Susan, started to put the sweets and coins back into the little pouch. Michael was clearly disappointed but was starting to feel better about not taking a sweet.

'Can we get some bonbons today Dean?' he asked.

'Definitely, I fancy some myself,' he replied.

The children made their way back inside. It felt good to be doing something honest and there was a real excitement at handing it in. Approaching the desk, they noticed the new receptionist. It was time to set up watch on the door again.

'We've found this in the play area,' said Pauline, lifting it up onto the desk.

'We think it belongs to Maddison,' Susan informed him.

'Thank you,' said the young man, dressed smartly in a navy blue waistcoat and white shirt. 'I'll telephone the office,' he said, picking up the phone.

'We'll wait here,' said Dean, choosing an ideal spot to keep watch on the door.

After five minutes, Maddison appeared holding Mr Fishwick's hand, hopping gently side to side with each step he took. Mr Fishwick's beard was nearly as long as Maddison's, and they actually looked alike, Susan noticed with a smile. The monkey was indeed missing his pouch. His rounded belly was now more noticeable, probably due to all the sweets he ate. Goodness knows what state his teeth are in, she wondered. His eyes passed along each child's face as they all stared in wonder, he was so well behaved.

'Now then Maddison, it looks like our little friends here have something of yours,' said Mr Fishwick to Maddison. Pauline handed the little red bag to the majestic monkey. He then began to jump up and down, making noises of obvious joy. He placed his long furry hand into the pouch and pulled out a bonbon, which he quickly put into his mouth. The loud, sucking sound made everyone laugh out loud.

'There's seventy pence in there as well as the sweets, Mr Fishwick,' said Susan, in an attempt to let him know they hadn't taken any.

'Ah yes, that's what we use to buy Maddison's sweets with once a month. He likes to hear it jangle when he runs. Thank you for finding it and handing it in. Shake everyone's hand Maddison,' commanded Mr Fishwick. Gently obeying his owner, Maddison tickled everyone with his thumb, as his soft hand touched the children's. Pauline tied the pouch back around his waist with a treble knot to make sure it didn't come off easily again. Maddison put his hand into the pouch and took out one sugar bonbon. He offered it to Michael who took it gleefully, glad more than ever now that he hadn't taken one earlier.

'How many bonbons does he eat a day?' asked Dean, as Maddison offered a sweet to everyone in turn.

'Oh, we buy him a pound and a half a week, and by Friday he'll be down to his last one, which he'll save until he gets his next bag.'

Mr Fishwick explained he had lots to do and turned to go through the kitchen doors. As he did, Maddison did a wiggle at the youngsters, then turned to join him. Dean had calculated that about now would be a good time for them to enter the door as well. Pauline's heart had already begun to beat faster at the thought. Two people were stood at the desk checking in.

'Are you sure now is the best time?' she questioned, in an attempt to get a delay.

'Oh Peewee,' sighed Susan, moving towards the doors, 'we're only going for a look around!'

In a flash, Dean and Michael were through, the receptionist seeing nothing. Susan grabbed Pauline's hand tight, having seen him bend down behind the desk, and in an instant, the flapping of the doors was the only sign that anyone had been in the area.

6

FORBIDDEN CORRIDORS

Once through, the girls were beckoned by Dean to quickly climb the stairs and join them. The noise of clattering didn't delay this request. At the top of the stairs, the world seemed a quieter place. The dark, dingy corridor smelt musty. The wallpaper was coming off, splitting large, red roses in half as it did. The landing seemed to stretch forever in the darkness, until it hit a small window at the bottom of the corridor, just gently lighting a passageway. The children explored further.

'Doesn't it feel old?' remarked Susan, looking in close at the décor on the walls.

'Apparently, my Mum says this part of the hotel hasn't been used since the forties,' said Dean, his eyes catching the sight of the yellowing coving around the ceiling edges.

'Why?' asked the girls in unison.

'Money, my Dad reckons,' he replied. 'A structural fault in the walls has made it unsafe,' he went on.

'Oh, it couldn't fall down, could it?' asked Pauline, becoming nervous again.

'Any minute,' Dean joked, arousing a laugh from Susan and Michael.

'I think most of these doors are locked,' said Susan, trying a couple of handles.

'Look here,' said Michael, as his eyes got used to the dimness, 'another lift.'

'It doesn't look as nice as the other one,' chirped Pauline, looking it up and down in the greyness. Susan came over for a better look.

'Designed and installed by Ernest Graves Otis,' she managed to read on the plaque above the wooden doors.

'It's an old service elevator,' said Dean, running his hand over the grey metal slats guarding the doors. 'It's not likely to work after all this time,' he continued, 'probably only reaches this wing of the hotel.'

'Most lifts don't work most of the time,' quipped Susan, peering through the glass windows into the darkness.

Pauline, now growing in confidence, travelled on towards the end of the corridor, a slit of light from under each doorway guiding her along. She noticed a curtain covering the window and pulled it to one side. Although the glass was dirty with fresh bird poo, the outward view of the sea was breath-taking. For a moment, Pauline's imagination was caught with the fact that none of the guests would ever enjoy this particular scene, the incoming sunshine chasing away the eeriness. As the others joined Pauline to look out of the window, they all heard a series of sounds. A rumbling then a thud, followed by what seemed like a vacuum cleaner in the distance. Dashing over to the lift, thoughts of, 'it does work but who's in it?' and where are they going?' chased through each of their minds. Pauline said what everyone was thinking.

'Oh no, Mrs Fishwick's heard us, and she's on her way up to get us,' voiced Pauline, rushing to the top of the steps, ready to make a quick getaway, with Michael following close behind. Susan and Dean stood rooted to the spot, partly due to fear and a burning curiosity. Would it stop at their floor or go up further?

With the curtain quickly drawn back in place, the darkness returned. If it did stop on the first floor, they felt confident of escaping quickly. Holding their breath quite still, they watched the arrow at the top of the doors move from 'B' to 'G'. With feet turned at the ready should it come any higher, the explorers held their nerve and stayed put, positioning themselves to catch a glimpse of whoever was in the lift, from a bird's eye view. The arrow started to pass 'G'. A faint light illuminated the travelling box. As it passed upwards, Susan caught sight of a dark blob with a flash of red and green. Dean was more observant, and noticed soft green eyes flick upward directly into his, hiding in the darkness. He instinctively jumped backwards, giving the others a scare.

'I think it's Maddison in the lift,' he declared, catching his breath as the lift passed the first floor.

'I thought so too, although I couldn't be sure,' added Susan, her heart beating wildly. Suddenly, the lift stopped at floor three, then started to descend again. Confirming what he saw as he passed by again, Dean gestured to Pauline and Michael, still crouched at the top of the stairs, to join them.

'It was Maddison and he was on his own,' babbled Dean.

'Yes, I saw him too when he went down again,' Susan confirmed, excitedly.

'Why was he in the lift alone?' asked Michael, now looking a little less frightened.

'Yeah, but what's on floor three?' said Pauline, ever curious, and now a little more settled in the darkness.

'He didn't stop to get out, there wasn't time, maybe he just likes rides,' Susan guessed, in an attempt to solve the mystery.

'I say we nip upstairs for a look,' dared Dean, with a mischievous grin, not fully seen in the absence of light.

All agreed. The staircase was wrapped around the lift in a 'C' shape. It was very difficult to mark out the line of each step. The carpet, which covered the old staircase, muffled the eight arms and legs clumping unrhythmically on upwards. By the time the four had felt their way to the top of the second flight, it was obvious they could go no further in the gloom. A briefing was called. 'Are we all here?' Dean inquired, as he turned to sit on the top step.

'Yep, although how we'll get down, I don't know,' replied Susan, turning to join Dean. It was quite scary in the dark, being where they shouldn't be. No-one was quite sure where to look as they discussed the options.

'We're not giving up, are we?' said Dean, keen to explore further.

'No, but we definitely need some kind of light,' Susan answered, Pauline now resting at her feet.

'Dean I've got my Glow Gob in my pocket, we could all wear a bit, so we could see where we are in the dark, suggested Michael excitedly.

'Oh, it's great, Glow Gob, I have loads all over my bedroom, my Mum's gone ape at all the mess, but you've got to get light on it first before it will glow,' she reminded him.

'Could you use matches?' asked Michael.

'No, it's far too dangerous – and you'd better not have any,' he said. Young Michael felt uncomfortable as the darkness hid the truth from his big brother.

'I bet my Dad will have brought his torch with him,' said Susan, glad to hear Dean talking sense.

'Why?' said everyone, puzzled.

'To find his way to the toilet in the night,' giggled Susan. 'Honest, he thinks of everything. It'll be in case there's a power cut or a fire in the night, so he can lead us all to safety.'

'Blimey!' exclaimed Dean, 'that's what you call planning!'

'We're always having power cuts at home, and the house across the road burned down one night. It's all given him a fright, so he likes to be prepared. I slept through the whole thing as well,' she exclaimed. 'The man across the road was only saved by his dog waking him up, and he ran down the street with no clothes on,' she added, laughing.

Temporarily defeated, the four carefully made their way back to the first floor, shuffling down each step. It was decided on the way down, that they would get the right equipment and return later that evening. Passing the elevator again, Pauline looked up at the floor indicator to see where Maddison had got out. She then realised something. The lowest level was 'B', yet on the main lift in Reception, it only began at 'G'. Telling the others, they discussed the fact that there must be a secret level that you could only reach in this lift, as the steps didn't go any further down.

'We've got to go down and have a look,' egged Susan, relieved at last that she could now see where she was going.

'Let's get out of here first,' whispered Dean, as he crept cautiously to the ground floor.

This was going to be hard. They had no idea who was watching on the other side of the door. Hearts raced faster. Susan, greatly known for her cheek, had an idea.

7

THE MYSTERY DEEPENS

'All follow me,' Susan announced. 'We're going straight into the kitchens.' Three faces of puzzlement followed Susan into the busy preparation area. 'Oh, so this is where all the food is made!' she said loudly, innocently looking around the large, steam-filled room with its white painted walls. Pauline quickly caught on to Susan's game.

'Yes, I told you they'd have at least five people working in here.' This suddenly became fun. Dean marched up to a young man dressed completely in white.

'We've come to see what's for tea,' he inquired of him.

'Well, err…,' he began, only to be interrupted by Mrs Fishwick's familiar voice.

'We do have menus young man, plus a blackboard in Reception with all the days' details on it,' she said sternly. 'It's against our rules to have anyone other than kitchen staff in here.'

'Sorry,' said Susan politely, 'but we just wanted to see all aspects of a real live, busy hotel. Pauline's interested in becoming a chefess when she's older, you see.'

'Err yes,' replied Pauline quickly, 'it's one of my choices.'

'Are you indeed?' replied Mrs Fishwick, her face softening. 'There's no such thing as a cheffess by the way,' she informed them in teacher mode, 'and you really must leave this area. Unfortunately, you've not got the right shoes on.'

They continued to ask questions about the kitchens as she led them out, past the service lift and into the reception area. Dean asked what they used the old lift for. She replied that they didn't, because it only reached the old part of the hotel, and then, quite surprisingly, informed them that it didn't work and hadn't done since the start of the First World War.

Susan quickly slapped her hand over Michael's mouth, as he attempted to blurt out what they had all just seen. Back in Reception, they chatted away at that afternoon's exciting events. 'We did see the lift working, didn't we?' queried Susan, immediately relieved at Dean's nod.

'We all heard it move up and down,' confirmed Pauline.

'This is very strange,' he said. 'How can we see it working plainly, with a monkey riding up and down, and Mrs Fishwick not think it's worked since the start of the war?'

'Is this what you call a mystery?' asked Michael, his eyes lighting up at the older children's excitement.

As the rain, now becoming a familiar part of the holiday, continued to pour down, the children decided to meet up in the TV lounge after dinner. The dining room was full of hungry people, chatting away about the day's events. 'What did you get up to this afternoon, then?' queried Mrs Watson, as she spooned mashed sprouts into baby John's mouth.

'Oh, this 'n that,' said Susan, guarding her reply, as she shuffled her sprouts around her plate.

'We'll be going shopping again tomorrow, being Monday, and Pauline… I've a nice surprise for you!' exclaimed Mrs Watson. Pauline's eyes lit up in response to hearing her Mum had sent some money to spend on clothes.

'Great, are we going in the morning or the afternoon?' she asked.

'Oh, all day, I shouldn't wonder,' replied Susan's Mum. 'The next town has one of those new shopping precincts. There aren't many like it in the country, we should be able to get something we don't usually see, eh?' The girls tried not to look disappointed. They were more excited about exploring the hotel than shopping, normally a favourite pastime.

Just then, Dean came over to the table. 'Hello,' he said, nodding quite shyly at Mr and Mrs Watson. 'About tonight…' he began, looking straight at Susan and Pauline. 'My Uncle Rupert has arrived, and Michael and I are expected to spend the evening with him.' The disappointment rang in his voice. 'So we'll see you tomorrow, after breakfast, eh?' he enquired. Mrs Watson, detecting despondence in the air, quickly reassured the girls that they had all week to go shopping.

'Ok,' they both replied, still deflated about having to put off tonight's exploration.

Dean returned to his table, his shoulders drooping, indicating his frustration about the revised evening. All of a sudden the holiday became boring! There was nothing good on the telly and neither girl enjoyed board games, as Mr Watson would always cheat, especially at Monopoly. 'Don't look so dejected because you can't play with your little friends,' said Mr Watson, 'you can watch me play snooker, if you like.' Pauline giggled at the suggestion.

'We can entertain ourselves, Dad,' declared Susan, finishing off the last of her delicious apple crumble.

'We may be able to play with Maddison, if we ask,' suggested Pauline, brightly.

'Oh, good idea, Peewee,' said Susan, with renewed excitement. 'We may even be able to feed him. May we leave the table?' The request granted, Susan and Pauline eagerly made their way to Reception to ask about Maddison, only to be told that he only ate once a day at breakfast, and because he was a very messy eater, it was always in private.

'Oh, blimey!' sighed Pauline 'we can't do that, the beach is wet through, Dean and Michael are with their Uncle all night, what can we do that's really good?'

'Let's go back to our room, get some chocolate and have a think,' replied Susan, taking charge. Chocolate was always good! As they opened the door to their room, a crinkling sound could be heard. Looking down, they saw a white piece of paper, neatly folded in two. Opening it quickly, the capital letters read

SECRET FEAST AT TEN O'CLOCK TONIGHT. MEET AT OLD SERVICE ELEVATOR ON FLOOR ONE. YOU BRING THE CHOCOLATE. CONFIRM BY STUFFING OLD CHOC WRAPPPER UNDER OUR DOOR.

P.S. BRING A TORCH!

8

IT ALL BEGINS TONIGHT

'Oh no, do you think we should?' said Pauline, nervously.

'Hmmm, I know what you mean,' replied Susan, looking in the bin for a discarded wrapper. 'Mum 'n Dad will expect us to be in bed with lights out, and we'd be seen at once going through the doors at that time.'

'It would be rather exciting though,' Pauline giggled, her confidence growing after the afternoon's adventure. With a deep breath, Susan agreed.

It took the boredom of the evening right away, and focussed their attention on planning the night ahead. Susan promptly ate a Walnut Whip, to provide the wrapper of confirmation needed. Depositing it under the door of 204 as instructed, Susan and Pauline went down to Mr and Mrs Watson's room, where her parents were getting ready to go down to the bar. There was a country singer on tonight and they wanted good seats. Unfortunately, baby John was being a pain. Well, this is how his big sister viewed it. The little chap was only eight months old. He didn't understand the need for a good seat and wanted to play some more. Susan suddenly surprised her parents. 'You go down, Peewee and I will get him off to sleep,' she announced, ever so sweetly.

'For a small fee, I suppose?' quipped Mr Watson.

'No, absolutely free of charge!' she exclaimed. Mrs Watson knew a good deal when she saw one.

'Come down with the key when he's gone off to sleep, and we'll let the baby-sitting service know,' smiled her Mum, leaving the room ultra-pleased at being able to secure one of the best spots to watch the cabaret. With the door closed, Susan instructed Pauline to get on with the lullabies while she looked for her Dad's torch. John's gurgles soon died down, and with the torch safely tucked away in her room, Susan presented the key and a full report to her thankful parents.

'Will it be late tonight, Mum?' asked Susan, in an attempt to plan around their return.

'No, not really,' she replied, looking at her watch. 'It's 7.30 now, the singer comes on just before 9pm. We'll look in on you about eleven o'clock, if you like?'

'Oh…err…no Mum,' Susan stumbled. 'Pauline and I are quite tired. After a spell in the study, we'll be going up to read and chat at nine o'clock, probably asleep for ten,' she explained, desperately trying to avert her Mum from looking in on them later.

'Oh, Ok love, the children's club is back on tomorrow, perhaps that will be a bit more exciting, eh?' Turning around to leave after kissing her parents good night, Susan began to smile at Pauline, only to scowl two seconds later, as she heard her Mum promise to pop her head around the door at eleven, just to make sure they were alright.

'Drat, why does my mum have to have a key to our room?' she whispered.

Both girls began to feel nervous as they headed out of the bar. It was bad enough creeping around the place, without having an eleven o'clock deadline to get back for.

'Perhaps it would be better calling it off?' suggested Pauline.

'Hmmm, let's see if we can find Dean and let him know,' replied Susan. After a search, neither Dean nor his family could be found in any of the leisure rooms. Then Pauline noticed their keys hanging up behind the receptionist, which meant they'd gone out for the evening.

'Let's go and look in the study and look in some of the books. You can see the entrance easily from there, and we'll tell him when we see him come back in,' suggested Susan.

Many of the books in the study were about Marlingham. One was placed on the centre table. It went into great detail about the fountain. Mrs Fradd had told the story quite adequately. The book also explained how the key was designed as several pieces, which locked together. Very special people were invited to piece the key together in a wonderful ceremony, just before the switch on. As the girls read together, they thought it was a great shame that Monsieur Lavadan had died in an epidemic.

'Thank goodness we have drugs to prevent big outbreaks like that,' said Pauline. 'It's a pity he didn't make two keys,' she went on. 'It says he died two years before it was stolen.'

Susan then discovered something Grandma Fradd had not told them. Quoting from the book, she read, 'On the night of the theft, many of Marlinghampton's citizens had seen a strange person, dressed in a black top hat and coat that had long tails, which hung almost to the floor. He carried a black stick, which he was seen waving about. He was seen around the fountain area and The Seafield Hotel! Many people came forward to try and identify him, but he disappeared as quickly as he came,' she finished. They discussed who might have done such a thing to pass the time.

Later on, other children began to gather, as Mr Fishwick brought Maddison in to have a question and answer session. Minutes soon turned to hours. It was ten to nine already and neither of them had noticed Dean and his family return.

The sound of laughter had begun to ring around the ground floor. The comedian was just starting his routine. The noise suddenly bellowed out, as the doors to the bar swung open. It was Mr Watson. The baby-sitting service had notified him that baby John was crying. He glanced in the study as he passed, and saw the girls engrossed in books and magazines. 'Susan,' he shouted from around the door, 'I think it's time you two went up to your room, you can read from there.'

'Drat,' Susan uttered under her breath. All attempts to delay the inevitable became futile, with a close call to a clip around the ear. As slowly as possible, the girls began to move, hoping any minute, that Dean would walk through the door and a signal to abort tonight's mission could be given. But no such luck. Back in their room, the girls became worried. Letting people down wasn't in their nature.

'Oh, he'll see the wrapper, go, and we won't be there at all,' said Pauline, wringing her fingers.

'Look, Dean said meet at ten,' declared Susan. 'Maybe we can catch him coming out of his room and explain then.' Thinking about it further, Susan then calculated that they could probably get to the lift, have a chocolate bar and get back to the room before eleven. They would just have to wait until tomorrow to do the exploring. Pauline agreed with the plan, but started praying secretly that they would see him on the stairs first.

'We'd better do the false 'in bed' routine again. Have you brought your Mr Tedd?' Susan asked. The black and blonde teddies were excellent substitutes for hair popping out of the top of beds. A few things stuffed under the bedclothes and, hey presto, two girls fast asleep. Well, it would look like that in semi-darkness. It had worked before when the girls had had a midnight feast at the bottom of the garden last year.

'Did you notice S, that Reception was quite quiet?'

'Yes,' replied Susan, 'I think it will probably be easier than we thought to nip through those doors. If anyone asks what we're doing, we'll say we're going to see Mum 'n Dad.'

Both girls' hands became sticky as they waited for 9.45 to come around. With hair tied back, and a torch hidden inside Susan's baggy, knitted cardigan, they carefully opened the door and cautiously stepped into the silent corridor. They quickly reached the top of the stairs. As they leaned over the bannister edge, the coast seemed clear. The comedian and singer had made the girl's task of entering the staff doors very easy. The rest of the hotel was feeling very empty and unlived in. As Susan and Pauline started down the final set of steps, the laughter could be plainly heard from the bar. Peeping around the corner, they could see the evening receptionist straining his ears to hear the jokes, his chuckles echoing around the reception area. With another peep around the corner showing the area clear, they kept low, creeping behind the large, plain white, leather settees, towards the kitchen doors.

In a flash, they had entered and began to climb the stairs. It was much darker now, as the lights in the kitchen were subdued for the evening. Susan duly switched on the torch. The batteries were low, and barely enough light shone to light the way up the dark stairway. 'I wish I'd checked it,' sighed Susan, annoyed at herself. 'This is only gonna last about five minutes.'

'It's enough to get us to the top of the first flight, and that's as far as we're going, isn't it?' said Pauline, encouragingly. Somehow, everything felt safe. Even though they were in a forbidden area, they felt calm. Susan began to whisper quite loudly.

'Dean…Dean, are you here yet?' she questioned the darkness. No sound could be heard. Both girls went and sat by the lift. Susan switched off the torch to save the battery, as they began to wait in the blackness.

'Time is now, Peewee?' asked Susan.

'Five past ten,' said Pauline, her Timex watch still illuminated. 'Suppose Dean's not got back with his family?' Pauline went on, 'I think we should leave if he's not here by quarter past.'

'Agreed,' answered Susan. 'We've got to get to be back in our room, snoring, by eleven.'

'I'm having my Walnut Whip now,' said Pauline. The waiting seemed to build tension in the pair.

'What time is it now P, can you still…'

'What was that click?' interrupted Pauline.

'What click? I didn't hear a thing,' said Susan, anxiously.

'I know I heard a noise from further along the corridor,' Pauline retorted loudly, forgetting to whisper.

'Shh,' said Susan, moving on to her feet. 'Someone may hear.' Both girls then noticed green lights dancing around, ahead of them. As the lights got nearer, the girls froze in fear. Every instinct told them to run down the stairs. It was suddenly all over with a 'BOO!' Switching on the torch, there was Dean's mischievous grin. His jumper was covered in tiny pieces of Glow Gob.

'I knew it was you,' said Susan, relieved that it was.

'So did I,' quipped Pauline. 'How long have you been there?'

'Since five to ten,' replied Dean, then promptly asking for a chocolate bar. 'Look here,' he said, pointing to the lift. 'The doors are open. Let's sit in here, we'll be able to talk a bit louder.' Sliding back the wooden doors, they crept in and closed the doors behind them.

'We've to be back for eleven,' Susan informed Dean. 'So we'll not have time to explore tonight.'

'Your torch isn't going to last more than five minutes,' said Dean, as the torch began to dim even more.

'I know,' she replied, 'my Dad will have brought batteries, I just forgot to check first!'

'Where's Michael?' asked Pauline, aware he wasn't hiding in the dark.

'Oh, he's got to be in bed earlier, and I thought it best not to bring him. Besides, he always gets giddy when he's excited,' Dean replied, popping the last of his chocolate bar in his mouth. Even though they could talk and eat chocolate anywhere, it was so much more exciting late at night in the lift. The talk went on, stories and jokes swapped endlessly for a good half hour. As the stories began to be interrupted with yawns from all three, they decided to make tracks back.

9

UH HOOO CHUNGO!

The torch had just started to flicker. 'Can you shine it over here?' said Dean, 'I can't see properly to open the door.'

'Sure,' said Susan, kneeling up.

'Can you see the handle?' Dean asked Pauline.

'Yep,' replied Pauline confidently, as she leaned over to put her fingers in the metal moulded handle.

'Which way does it slide?' she asked, puzzled. 'I thought it slid over to the left?'

'Let me try,' said Susan, 'hold the torch P, maybe you've to press a catch at the same time or something. Can either of you see anything?'

Try as they might, somehow those doors weren't budging. Pauline began to panic.

'We've got to be back in twenty minutes,' she reminded them, uneasily.

'How on earth did this thing shut, I thought you closed it ajar?' said Susan, knowing all too well that her Dad would cancel all spending money until Christmas if she was caught disobeying him. Dean's hands began to sweat as he pulled on the handle. The torch began to flicker erratically. Susan began to shake it. As it tipped up to the ceiling, the battery must have made a better connection, and the light became stronger. All three had felt around the door area. There had to be something to pull, push or move.

'It's probably a safety thing,' said Dean, trying not to sound worried. 'We'll find it in a mo.'

'Ohh, I suddenly feel all claustrophobic,' said Susan, dramatically.

'So do I,' said Pauline. 'What if we're stuck here all night?

'We can't shout for help, 'if we do we'll be in real trouble,' Dean reminded them.

The girls started to feel upset. Their faces gave nothing away in the dimness, but Dean could hear it in their voices as they began to consider what to do. The torchlight shone to the roof of the lift. As the light cascaded down the lift walls, Susan noticed little flags, which pointed to each floor. She began to wonder how these old lifts had worked. Dean interrupted her thoughts by announcing he had an idea. Noticing a square in the ceiling, he had worked out that if the lift ever got stuck, there had to be an emergency way out. 'If we can open that trap door, I can climb up and get out onto the next floor up.'

'Oh, do you think you could?' asked Pauline, hopefully. 'Won't it be dangerous? she added.

'I can shine the torch onto the Glow Gob on my jumper, maybe it will illuminate the lift shaft a little bit?' suggested Dean. 'But first of all, how can I get up there?'

Susan had noticed an oblong edging where she had seen the little flags sticking out. Peering in closer, it said 'pull'. Doing just that, down came the green leather seat, falling just to the left of the trap door. 'Hey, that's great,' said Dean, impressed with Susan's discovery. 'An adult would be able to reach easily,' he observed. 'I'm going to need a leg up.'

'You'd better come back for us,' demanded Susan, realising they'd only known this boy for twenty four hours. Cupping their hands, Susan and Pauline created a step. With all their strength, they raised him upwards towards the trap door. Dean took the torch and shone it on the trap door, revealing some kind of indented handle. All of a sudden, the human steps collapsed, causing him to tumble on the girls.

'I'm sorry,' said Susan, 'I'm not very strong. I've a better idea to lift you up though,' she said, rubbing her sore fingers. Susan placed her arms on top of the newly found seat, grabbing it securely at its edges. Her back formed a much steadier platform. Pauline helped him up and held the torch, leaving both of Dean's hands free to get a good grip.

'Found it,' he shouted back, excitedly.

'Shh,' came back the reply.

'Sorry,' whispered Dean, 'but I've found it.'

'Good, now get up there, my back's killing me,' said Susan, starting to fidget. Dean removed the lid and hoisted himself through, his gymnastic abilities giving him the edge. He whispered back loudly, 'it's too dark, can you pass me the torch through for a minute?'

Susan straightened up as Pauline stood on the green leather seat, and stretching out, passed their only light source through the hole. 'Hey, you're not taking that with you,' exclaimed Susan, forgetting to whisper as it went pitch black inside the lift. Dean looked carefully at the structure of the lift shaft. It was quite a way to the next floor up and he would need light to see where he was going. 'I'm going to need you to shine the torch up into the lift shaft,' he said. 'I can see the next floor, but it's a climb.'

Susan asked Pauline if she would be the backbone this time and she would shine the torch up, which was getting dimmer by the minute, to guide Dean's escape. Balancing on a beam four inches wide seemed easier than balancing on Pauline's back in the darkness, but somehow the will to get out of the lift brought confidence. Susan, after checking with Pauline to see if she was still ok, asked Dean where exactly he wanted the light to shine.

'Towards the next door up,' he said confidently, 'can you see where I mean?'

The shaft smelled musty with the years of dampened dust. It felt eerie to Dean as he stumbled to find a handhold. If the second floor had been lit up, the task would have been much simpler. To the corner of the shaft were several pipes; these would make good footholds. Back in the lift, the girls could hear footsteps exploring the roof.

'Is he there yet?' asked Pauline wearily, now fully appreciating Susan's earlier moan of backache.

'He's in the corner,' replied Susan, 'that's all I know. I hope he knows what he's doing. I wouldn't do it for a week of Walnut Whips!'

'Susan…' said Pauline, in a worried voice. 'If we don't get out, and your Mum spots it's not us in bed, we'll be in super trouble, and she'll tell my Mum that I've not behaved, she'll ground me, and I'll not see you for the rest of the year!'

'He's just got to do it. I hope that he doesn't just go to his room to get us back for laughing at him on the first day!'

'Mrs Fishwick may not even let us stay, if she finds out what we've been up to!' Pauline sighed.

'Peewee!' Susan exclaimed, 'let's not worry about what might never happen. We'll get out, ok?' trying to calm her in the dark. Susan shouted up to Dean in the darkness, 'have you made it?'

'Nearly,' came back the strained reply. 'I've got a hold on the bottom of the metal guards on the next floor up, keep the torch still!' The torch started to dim at Dean's last words.

'Oh no, it's going! Can you still see?' asked Susan, hopefully.

'Not a blinking thing!' gasped Dean, in the blackness. The light was finally gone. It started to get scary. He had hold of the guard, but needed to steady himself on the wall to help him scrape up. In the darkness, he couldn't see where to put a foot, apart from where his mind had last memorised, and was now dangling nine feet up from the lift roof.

To fall now would be disastrous; he had to get up somehow. Using all his strength, he attempted to lift his legs to the level of his hands, and lie perched on the doorway edge, a space only six inches wide. Dean's upper arms, aching from hanging for the last five minutes, now started to give him pain. His fingers were locked around the metal guard, its square bars not giving him a comfy grip. With one almighty swing, he did it, managing to catch his foot half in one of the bars, giving extra hold. Dean breathed out at the temporary relief. By now, he was exhausted and unsure of his next move. Suddenly, but gently, in the darkness came a long arm, wrapping itself around the young boy's body. A voice in the darkness said, 'let your feet fall while I pull you safely to the edge.' Dean obeyed the instruction without fear. At the same time, the metal guard was drawn aside and another arm then pulled him to safety on the second floor.

Meanwhile, the girls were sat in silence. Each going through a worst case scenario of stern talks, groundings and no spends. Eyes were watering; each of them knowing it was well past eleven. The lift doors slid open without warning, making them jump.

'Dean?' Susan queried in the darkness.

'I'm here,' he said, shaken by his ordeal, but relief clearly in his voice. The lift suddenly lit up, its brightness forcing everyone to hide his or her eyes for a second.

Before them stood Maddison, taller and straighter than he usually did. 'Come with me,' he said, in a clear and powerful voice. The girls gasped in amazement. Then for a moment felt afraid. 'Don't be alarmed,' gestured Maddison, detecting their fear, as he held out his hand reassuringly. The girls quickly rose to their feet, still aware that eleven o'clock had passed, and there was more trouble to face. Yet here they were, with a monkey who talked. Were they dreaming?

Dean suddenly burst into frenzied conversation, 'Maddison just saved me in the lift shaft!' he exclaimed, excitedly, 'he knows you've to be back in your room by eleven, and he knows a quick way back.'

Still stunned by what had just happened, Susan and Pauline followed Dean and Maddison back up two flights of stairs, which were now lit up by soft green lights fixed to the walls. They approached what looked like a broom cupboard, just to the left of the lift. Maddison instructed them to walk through, pushing the back of the wall. This would lead to the store cupboard located on each floor of the main hotel. As Dean stayed behind, he swore them to secrecy about hearing Maddison speak, and told them he'd catch them in the morning. Quickly following the instructions given, the girls found themselves on the landing opposite room 411.

'Brilliant,' cried Susan, fumbling for her key. As they entered the room, they half expected to see the light on, with Mr Watson sat on the bed, tapping a stick in his hand, just like the one kept at the home for disobedient girls and boys, above the picture in the lounge. Fortunately, the threat of it had prevented Susan ever feeling it on her behind.

All was dark and it felt chilly. The pillows and teddies, still arranged in disguise. 'Quick Peewee, get undressed and into bed, in case they come,' Susan uttered, as she began ripping off her clothes.

'I can't see my pyjamas,' Pauline squealed.

'They're under your pillow, I think,' was the distracted reply. 'Shh!' exclaimed Susan, listening intently. The sound of voices could be heard, getting nearer and more familiar. Instinctively, both girls dived into bed, half dressed, hearts beating frantically. The comedian had obviously given a good show. Mr and Mrs Watson were in excellent mood, repeating some of the good punch lines to regain the sensation of laughter.

It all went quiet for a few seconds. The bedroom door opened quietly. A head popped through the frame, the silence was unbearable. A bout of nervous laughter was about to cross the room from Pauline's bed, when the door closed as silently as it had opened. Only when it was certain all was clear, did Susan and Pauline let out the biggest gasp of air imaginable.

'I hope there's not a fire alarm tonight P,' said Susan, laughing with relief as she pulled her Dad's torch out from under the bedclothes.

Talk of the night's adventure went on into the early hours of the morning, both girls recounting each thrilling moment. Did they really hear the monkey speak? How did Maddison know they'd to be back by eleven? Question after question was repeated furiously, until slowly but surely, the pause between each sentence got longer and longer, as both girls drifted off into sleep.

10

THE MYSTERY BEGINS TO UNRAVEL

Tuesday morning came in a jiffy. The sun, ever first to rise, had just begun to peep through a crack in the curtains, directing its rays on the corner of Pauline's bed, signalling a time of somewhere between eight and eight fifteen. Mrs Watson entered the room, singing merrily, with baby John in her arms.

'Rise and shine,' she echoed, as she plonked him on Susan's bed. His loud gurgles entered Susan's dream, which formed part of a roar of laughter coming from a big, black, burly gorilla, which was reading a book about earthworms, which were reading and writing backwards. The disturbance was more than enough to bring her back into the real world. But as she awoke, a sense of insecurity struck her at once. The night's encounter flooded back into her mind.

Her first words as she saw her Mum and Stinky were, 'that monkey can talk!'

'Really?' replied Mrs Watson, humouring her daughter. 'What can he say then?' she questioned, as she crossed the room to open the curtains fully.

'Come with me,' Susan replied, sleepily, and puzzled at why her Mum didn't react more surprised.

'You've been dreaming again, darling. That's a sign that you've had a good quality sleep,' she reassured her. 'Now, up you get or you'll miss breakfast – oh, you do look tired.'

Realising it was probably not wise to mention any more about last night's capers, Susan began to sit up slowly, and after kissing little John, attempted to wake Pauline, still in the deepest of sleeps. As Mrs Watson and John left the room, Susan perched herself on the end of her bed. With knees up to her chin, she began to shout over to Pauline, and at the same time, ponder her sanity. As Pauline started to awaken, she opened one eye only, fixing it on her pal.

'It's not really time to get up yet, is it?' came the moan.

'Yep,' announced Susan, fully awake.

'Oohhh S,' exclaimed Pauline loudly, as if a switch had just been flicked on in her brain, 'Maddison can talk!' She sat up to face her friend.

'Thank goodness *you've* said it!' replied Susan. 'I thought I'd been dreaming it. In fact, I told my Mum as soon as I woke up, but she didn't believe me.'

'Who would believe us?' stated Pauline, as she made her way over to the sink.

'Well, let's hope Dean knows what we're talking about, or we've both caught a madness bug!' said Susan, as she tried to find an uncrumpled T-shirt.

The girls then heard a small knock at the door. Pauline opened it slowly, peeping around the edge to see Dean smiling at her.

'Let me in,' he said, pushing the door forcefully. 'I've been knocking since seven o'clock,' he blurted out, excitedly. 'What a night, eh?' Both girls, unconcerned at being in a state of undress, began to question Dean about his encounter with Maddison. 'Look, I can see this isn't the best moment to reveal all. Can you meet me later this morning – say ten o'clock – outside in the children's play area?'

'Hopefully, I'll have to check with my Mum first that we aren't going shopping,' replied Susan. 'If not, we'll pop a note under your door just after breakfast. Now scoot, we need to get dressed, or we'll miss it.'

'OK,' he beamed, 'you're gonna be blown sideways when you hear what I've got to tell ya!'

Breakfast was a rather rushed affair. Mr and Mrs Watson, noticing that both girls missed out their cereals, started to harp on about being hungry later on. But Susan and Pauline had their minds on meeting Dean as soon as possible.

'I actually think I've been eating a bit too much since coming on holiday,' Susan said, trying to calm her Mum.

'Well, that's a new one!' exclaimed Mr Watson, 'more like leaving room for Mars bars, or whatever it is you stuff your face with.'

'It's Twix actually, Dad,' Susan corrected him, 'but we aren't going to fill up with anything – honest.'

As the girls left the dining room, with permission to meet Dean, Pauline admitted that she felt hungry and would probably need a Walnut Whip to fill the gap, like in the next thirty minutes. The sun had kept shining, so it was easy persuading the adults that they would be on the beach below for most of the day. Dean was already sat on the swing as the girls approached the play area.

'Hi,' was swapped by all three.

'We couldn't wait to get here,' Pauline announced, 'you haven't any chocolate, have you?' she added.

'She's not had enough breakfast, as you can tell,' Susan informed him.

'Listen, forget chocolate, Maddison wants us to meet him at the lift at eleven o'clock, but this time we'll go through the store cupboard to avoid being seen,' Dean pointed out.

'Have you had a proper conversation with him then?' asked Susan, disbelievingly. Although the girls recalled last night's events together, it was still hard to take in that a monkey could talk.

'He's just like you and me,' said Dean, sitting on the grass besides the girls. 'A long time ago, just after the turn of the century, a circus travelling the country stopped at Marlingham. The animals weren't treated very well and the Mayor at the time, Mr Francis somebody intervened, and …'

'Francis Eaves,' interrupted Pauline, the name familiar from Grandma Fradd's story and the books in the study at the hotel.

'Yeah, that's him, anyway, he intervened and rescued many of the ill-treated chimps and lions. He found good homes for all but one of the monkeys, and decided to keep it for himself. It was a female, called Chiquita, who was very good at doing tricks and things. So Mr Richmond, the owner of The Seafield Hotel, offered to buy her to amuse his guests. This worked very well until one day, she just disappeared into thin air. A reward was offered, but she was never found.

Then five years later, from nowhere, appeared a baby monkey, actually in the hotel grounds. Mr Richmond was besotted with it, and thought someone had placed it there to make amends for stealing the other one in 1903.

'Don't tell me,' said Susan, wide-eyed, 'he named him Maddison.'

'Sure did,' confirmed Dean, and he's lived here ever since. He's a very special monkey, and learned to speak from all the guests who came to stay, but NO-ONE, absolutely NO-ONE knows he can speak.'

Except us,' corrected Pauline, quickly.

'That's right,' nodded Dean, excitedly, 'and he's told me that he will tell us why he's blown his cover this morning.'

'Have you told Michael?' asked Susan.

'No way. Mighty mouth would have it all over town in twenty minutes,' he laughed.

'No-one will believe him,' said Susan, confidently. 'I told my Mum this morning as I woke up in a daze – she thought I was dreaming.'

'Probably,' said Dean, 'but Michael has a very honest face and never tells lies, so they would probably take him a bit more seriously.'

'Hmm, maybe,' agreed Susan, who was now also feeling a little bit hungry. After a secret visit to the tuck shop, the trio climbed the stairs to the second floor, and entered the cupboard leading to the disused part of the hotel.

Maddison greeted them as they stepped out. Still wearing his waistcoat, he actually looked different. His stance was more human, standing tall and straight. He stretched out his long arms, and gently took hold of each girl's hand to reassure them. His presence made them all feel at ease in the unused part of the hotel, as his soft, green eyes smiled back at them. A tender, but fatherly voice, spoke these words. 'Susan and Pauline, don't be alarmed. There are many things you don't know about the world, one of these things is that I can talk and think for myself. I can do this above any other animal on earth because I don't come from here.'

Many thoughts were running through their minds, but a deep sense of awe and respect prevented them from being spoken. It somehow didn't seem right to ask any questions. As Maddison led them into a room along the hallway, he continued, 'I told Dean to tell you about the circus monkey, Chiquita, going missing, and about the baby monkey who appeared about five years later – that baby being me.'

'Yes, thank you, he did. Is this your bedroom?' Susan asked, courteously. The room smelled sweet with lavender. Looking around, the children could see plain white walls, with an early picture of The Seafield hung above a bare fireplace. A small bed, with green and red blankets, neatly tucked in the sides, was practically the only furniture in the room. A thick, green patterned carpet covered the floor, with a red, wooden chair positioned by the window, which offered a cheery view of the sea and beachhead.

'I sleep in here, but most of the time, I'm with Mr and Mrs Fishwick about the hotel.'

'Your bedroom's much tidier than mine, Maddison,' confessed Pauline.

'And mine,' admitted Susan, with a laugh. Dean was giving nothing away. Apart from the tiny bit of furniture, the children noticed that Maddison had lots of little curios scattered about. Brightly coloured pots, painted red and green, sat on shelves in a corner, along with a range of old fashioned accordions and other musical instruments. Gold coloured pipes, and bits of obscure looking metal, were thrown in next to children's toys, well-worn and used by Maddison to entertain himself.

Now feeling more at ease, Dean felt he could ask him where he came from. Maddison gestured for them to sit on his bed. He began with a twinkle in his eye.

11

THE KEY TO IT ALL

'The old service elevator, is a hidden doorway to another place,' said Maddison.

'What kind of place?' said Susan, as she adjusted her position.

'Think of it as another world, except the people aren't like they are here.'

'What are they like?' interrupted Dean.

'It's hard to explain,' continued Maddison, 'but it's where I come from.'

'Are they all animals like you?' asked Pauline.

'No, a variety of people live there,' Maddison answered. He went on, 'your world and mine are always separated by the magic of science, but every once in a while the doorway can be opened. That's what happened to Chiquita.' Maddison seemed saddened as he continued, 'Chiquita was on the ground floor playing with a little girl. They both heard a strange noise coming from below the lift shaft. The girl, about seven years old, then reported that the lift doors opened and Chiquita got in, because she seemed to be following a strange smell she'd picked up. All of a sudden, the lift descended. The young girl waited for the monkey to come back. After a while, her curiosity got the better of her and she called the lift to find her little playmate, but she had disappeared. The girl told Mr Richmond exactly what she had seen, but the little monkey was never found.'

'Do you know what happened?' asked Dean, beating Susan and Pauline to the question.

'Vaguely,' answered Maddison. 'I was only a youngster when this female Chimpanzee was found crying on a small island in the middle of a nearby lake. She was brought back to the family camp and stayed, because we looked similar. The elders of our family tried to find out where she had come from, but she was unable to speak to us. We tried using sign language, and after a while Chiquita took us to a cave on the island where she was found.

'She never learned to communicate like us though, and the whole thing remained a mystery. I now know that the doorway opens automatically. This happens once every thousand Riva, that's how we measure our time, which here at The Seafield Hotel, counts the same as one of your years.' He carried on while the children listened in utter amazement. 'From our side, the doorway entrance is in the cave. On this side, it connects here to the basement of The Seafield. Access to anything here, can only be made if the lift goes down to the basement within a certain time period, which lasts twelve hours of your time.'

'Why didn't Chiquita come back?' asked Susan. At this point Maddison's eyes filled with tears.

'I played with her quite a lot because she was so different to us, cheerful and happy, but as the Rivas passed on, she became very quiet and hum-drum, like we were. Sadly, she became ill, and we were never able to figure out how to get her home to make her better. She seemed quite old, and one day she just didn't wake up.'

'Do you think she wanted to get home?' Pauline quizzed Maddison.

'I don't think she thought about it,' he replied. 'She brought a lot of joy to our family before she fell asleep.'

'So how come you're here then?' inquired Susan, shifting her position again.

'It was her brightness and playfulness that made me curious. For a time, she made ME feel happy and glad, and when she became like us, I was aware that I had lost something I had never had before. I wanted to experience that again. So I made a habit, every day, to visit the cave to see what I could find. What I didn't know, was that the lift had to be in the basement. Then one day, a few of your years later, it happened by accident. The lift had been sent down to the basement just at the right time period, and I got in and up I popped.

'Within minutes of arriving I felt happier, and regained those feelings I had when Chiquita was first with us. I worked out that she had picked up the smell of illandrium, coming from our world. It's a special flower which, when it gets warm, gives off a powerful scent. So I guess she got in to the lift to follow the trail. Somehow it got sent to the basement, and hey presto – she was in Abacus.'

'Is that the name of your world?' Susan asked.

'It was,' replied Maddison, cautiously, 'but then someone called Erasmus Drab mysteriously arrived, and soon became very powerful. After many Moons of his arrival, he decreed the city to change its name, to Drabacus, after himself.'

'What does decreed mean?' asked Susan.

'It's when someone orders something to be done,' said Maddison.

'Did nobody object?' cried Dean, at the cheek of the man.

'Somehow nobody did. Everybody, and this included my family as well, just agreed to his plans,' replied Maddison.

'Blimey, he must have been very domineering,' commented Pauline, 'things are usually decided by committees here. That seems much fairer.'

'Not quite everything,' Dean reminded her. 'What about the world wars we've had? My Granddad fought in the second one against someone who wanted to do what he wanted, called Adolf Hitler.'

'Yes – but Maddison said that nobody minded in this case. That is what you said, isn't it?' observed Susan, as she turned to Maddison for confirmation.

'That's right, Susan,' he nodded. 'Soon after his arrival, things started to get boring and uneventful, people lost their cheeriness, everyone was the same, not celebrating new additions to the family, not really caring anymore that things seemed different. I was so young that I didn't really remember what it was like before he came.'

'What a shame,' said Pauline, thoughtfully. 'I mean, it's not all excitement here all the time, but we're certainly not fed up all the time either.'

'Is that why you stayed, Maddison?' asked Dean, 'to feel happier?'

I wish I could say that's the only reason,' he replied, alarmingly.

'That Drab fellow might have died by now,' Susan announced, 'after all, this is many years ago.'

'I haven't been able to keep an accurate record because our methods of time keeping are different, but after I'd got used to it, I worked out that it all happened in the early nineteen hundreds. However...' he said, cautiously, 'no-one ever dies in Drabacus!'

'What?' cried all three children together.

'I know from what you understand about life, it might be a bit hard for you to take on board,' smiled Maddison, 'but, it's just normal to me.'

'Does that mean you'll never die, then?' said Dean, as his jaw dropped wide.

'I'm not sure,' Maddison frowned. 'Since I've been here, these last few years I have noticed a few aches and pains associated with old age.'

'Can't you go back to see if your aches and pains get better?' suggested Dean.

'I can, but I would probably feel dull and miserable within half a day or so. Besides, I have been back every year, and Drab is still commanding the city,' Maddison informed them.

'Does anyone else know how to get here?' Pauline asked, her head cocking to one side. Maddison went very quiet at this point. He looked almost ashamed.

'What's the matter?' asked Dean, softly.

One more person has visited,' Maddison confessed. 'When I came here for the first time, I didn't know it, but Erasmus Drab followed me.' Maddison's head fell towards his chest. 'I didn't know he was here until he appeared in the corridor. He didn't see me, but he was clutching something in his hand. He called the lift and went back to Drabacus.'

'What was it?' interrupted Pauline. At this point, Maddison got off his bed and collected something from the corner. All three heads turned to see him return with a piece of metal rod.

'This is part of what he carried,' he went on. 'I'd have never known what it was but for a young girl, who had seen Erasmus Drab commit a wicked thing – stealing. She saw him early in the evening, near the fountain. Noticing that he looked very different, as he does, she decided to keep an eye on him. Later on, she saw him leaving the area near the fountain pump house, with a large, misshapen object in his hand. He placed it under his long, black cloak and strode off, towards here. So she followed him, as far as the old service lift, and saw him disappear. Now, I saw her at this point, but didn't want to approach her because I could see she was frightened. I tried following him, but because I had waited for the little girl to go, by the time I called the lift, the door to

Drabacus had closed. However, over the next few days, the rumpus started about the fountain not working, and I wondered if Erasmus Drab had anything to do with it.'

'I bet he did,' cried Susan to the others, 'it sounds like HE pinched the key!'

'You're right, Susan,' confirmed Maddison. 'The girl came back several times to the lift entrance on the ground floor. By this time, Mr Richmond had taken me in, since I couldn't get back to Drabacus for a year, so I made friends with her. After a few visits, I felt I could confide in my new, young friend, the fact that I could talk.'

'Was she shocked?' asked Dean, remembering his own amazement at hearing Maddison speak.

'Just a little bit,' he replied, smiling. 'But like you three, soon forgot in the urgency of what I had to share. We became best friends.' Maddison passed the piece of metal to Dean. 'The thing that bonded us together was I discovered that SHE was the girl playing with Chiquita when she disappeared in the lift, which is why she'd become frightened when she saw Drab disappear in the same way. Ada, that was her name, told me what she'd seen that night when I saw him go back to Drabacus. From that moment, I knew I had to guard the lift to prevent him from ever returning and spoiling more things.'

'How can you do that?' said Dean, looking puzzled.

'By making the lift faulty and unable to travel to the basement. These old lifts were powered by hydraulics, and I learned how to shut off the water supply at the time the doorway is open. The engineers came out so often that they recommended to Mr Richmond that he install one of the new types, which worked by electricity, after the First World War.

'So now, you control the doorway,' stated Susan, excitedly.

'That's right, and he's never been able to return since. That's part of the reason I stay. To make sure he can't ever come here again. He wants to rob peoples' sparkle and spoil everything good and fresh about life. I feel responsible for your fountain falling into ruin.'

Maddison's story so far had taken the best part of the morning, and tummies had started to rumble in succession.

12

THE CHALLENGE

'Help yourselves to fruit,' Maddison offered, as Pauline's stomach made the loudest sound ever. The crunching of apples helped to silence the hunger pangs, as the three friends eagerly pestered Maddison for more answers.

'I wonder if this is part of the fountain key?' Susan thoughtfully said, as it passed into her hand for inspection, 'is there a picture of it?' Maddison reached for an old book on Marlingham, and turning to page nine, revealed a rough line drawing.

'Oh, it's definitely part of it,' pronounced Maddison to Susan and Pauline.

'Look here,' pointed out Dean, 'this is the bit that all the others click onto. It looks complicated.'

'Wow,' said Pauline, 'how did you come to get this bit and not the rest of it?'

'Ada, my young friend, was quite a gutsy character, and persuaded me to try and get it back,' he replied. 'We had to wait a year, visiting the basement every day, until the right time came around. We worked that out from the time Chiquita disappeared and I appeared. It was Ada who obtained the piece. I had to stay in the lift, to make sure it was in the basement, ready for her return. She was about your age by this time.'

'So she went on her own?' cried Susan, 'she was very brave!'

'Oh yes, she was, I couldn't have gone on my own,' said Pauline, sharing Susan's thoughts.

'Oh I could,' said Dean, cockily. Both girls turned, and silently mouthed 'big head', to each other.

'Well, that was the problem, actually,' said Maddison. 'Ada, nor any person, could enter Drabacus and not be affected by Drab's influence. That's why she didn't succeed in getting the whole key back, she wasn't strong enough.'

'How did she get this piece, then?' inquired Dean. Maddison's reply was concise.

'Ada met an old friend of mine, Mixy Lune. He told her he'd seen Erasmus Drab drop something as he'd hurried past him once. It was near the cave entrance. It all came apart as it hit the ground, and he just gathered up the bits, not noticing this piece that had rolled under some Delanthrium bushes. So this bit was easy!'

'Did she try to get the other pieces back?' asked Susan, as she held the six-inch key rod up to her eye.

'There were two pieces dropped by him. Ada kept the other, just in case he did ever manage to get back, should he discover he didn't have all the pieces. But she was unable to obtain any of the other key bits. Only after a few hours, she realised she felt different. I'd warned her of his controlling power, so she decided to return. Mixy was able to inform her though that Erasmus Drab headed up to the citadel with the other pieces.'

'What's a citadel?' asked Susan.

'You would call it a palace or castle here,' Maddison informed her.

'Couldn't you ask anybody else in your world to help out?' Pauline asked.

'I tried, while Ada held the lift in the basement, but I couldn't convince anyone to help.'

'Rotten lot,' snapped Dean.

'No, no,' Maddison was quick to correct him. 'They are all good people, but Erasmus Drab's influence makes them indifferent to everything.'

'What's indifferent mean?' asked Susan.

'Blimey!' said Dean. 'Do you not know anything?' Susan pulled her tongue at Dean.

'Indifferent means they just don't see a need to help, lack of interest.' He carried on, 'I think Ada and I could have found a way if we'd been together longer.'

'What happened?' Susan burst in first to ask. She was definitely in questioning mode.

'Within four weeks of her return from Drabacus, her father, who was in the army, was posted to London, and the family moved away. She sent me a postcard, but Mr Richmond didn't show it to me. I found it pinned to the notice board in Reception and read it. We lost touch after that. With the war and everything.

'You can read, that's excellent,' noted Pauline, excitedly.

'Hmm,' pondered Susan, 'so that explains why the fountain stopped working and why no-one had a hope of finding the key.'

'Did Ada never tell any adults, to see if they could get it back?' asked Pauline.

'Yes, we could have sent the army in for it,' said Dean.

'Ada told the story to her Mum and Dad, but they just wouldn't believe her,' replied Maddison.

'Surely this piece would have convinced them?' said Dean, getting agitated at the thought of nothing being done.

'Yeah, and if you'd talked...' began Susan, only to be interrupted gently by Maddison.

'I felt a conflict with Erasmus Drab was too dangerous for your world. What do you think would have happened if he'd secured passage here? Everyone would have lost interest in things and moped about, it happens to everyone. The First World War was about to break out in only a few years' time. Your army could have been made useless, and you might all be speaking German now,' he said, bringing home the reality of what that could have meant to the children. 'No,' said Maddison, confident that he had made the right decision, 'I knew a time would arrive when the right people could be relied upon.' Maddison's face told his thoughts.

Silence filled the room for a moment. Dean, Susan and Pauline each felt tingles as they realised, one by one, he meant them. Dean was the first to comment. 'So you think we three could get the key back from Drab?'

'Oh 'eck, I'm not so sure,' quivered Pauline, after all she'd heard. Susan boldly asked why Maddison thought they could succeed where he and Ada had failed.

'Because you will work as a team and help each other,' he replied. 'I saw evidence of this with the episode in the lift last night. Plus, I set a test with the sweets, to see if you were honest, and I felt sure when I met you, that you were. One of Drab's best weapons is temptation. Once he knows you're weak in an area, he'll use it to put you under his influence.'

'But how does this influence thing work?' Susan asked, puzzled.

'I'm still not one hundred percent sure about that,' admitted Maddison, 'but I'm confident my friend, Mixy Lune, knows something that could help you.'

'Well, I'm willing to have a go!' cried Dean, excitedly.

'Hmm, I'm a bit scared,' confessed Susan. Pauline's face revealed completely how she felt.

'I don't think I could do it,' Pauline announced. Maddison tried to reassure the girls.

'You don't need to go, and it has to be all of you, or none of you. This is an important part of the plan,' he said, gently.

'Oh, come on girls,' said Dean, 'just think of the adventure, and I'll look after you both!'

Susan turned to Pauline. 'I will if you will,' she said to Pauline, coaxingly. 'I mean, it's a bit mind-blowing. Just think of the essay we could write in next term's creative writing competition.' Pauline's mouth began to relax at the corners. 'Plus, just think about the reward! Five pounds would keep us in chocolate until the end of the summer!'

'Suppose we can't get back?' said Pauline, half warming to the idea. Maddison reassured her that Drabacus wasn't a big place, and he would make sure they would get back in time.

'Won't our parents miss us though?' queried Dean, sensibly.

'Well, here's another bit of science. Each time I've returned, I've noticed that time goes at a different pace to here. For instance, on my last visit, I spent a whole day there, and when I returned, only three hours had passed.'

'That's incredible,' cried Dean, amazed, quickly working out that eight days there was equal to one here. He was also good at Maths.

'Gosh, the whole thing sounds unbelievable,' said Susan. 'No wonder no-one believed little Ada. It's made my brain tired just thinking about it.'

'Er, when were you thinking of us going?' Pauline asked Maddison, slowly.

'Oh good on ya Peewee,' said Susan, congratulating her. 'You're gonna go then?'

'I suppose so,' she smiled, 'I won't hear the last of it if I don't!'

'That's true,' Susan confessed, smiling back.

'Well Maddison,' said Dean, 'when is the next time the lift can go to Drabacus?' Dean asked, excitedly.

'Well, I don't want to rush you,' he said, taking in a big gulp of air, and then smiling, 'but it's open from nine o'clock tonight until nine o'clock tomorrow morning!'

13

THE FIBS HAVE STARTED!

The morning had ticked on, the trio having agreed to meet Maddison when it was safe to do so, about ten o'clock that night. As they entered the reception area, Michael suddenly shouted to his brother, his tear-stained face revealing the pain of not being able to find anyone for the last couple of hours. 'Where have you all been?' he asked angrily, with disappointment in his voice.

'Nowhere,' fibbed Dean, feeling sorry for him.

'I've been looking all over for you,' he said, clearly fed up at being left out. 'You'd better not have been exploring without me!'

'Oh no, we've definitely not been exploring, it wouldn't be any fun without you,' said Pauline, attempting to make him feel better.

'Where have you all been then?' demanded Michael, as he stared at all three in turn.

'In our room, just chatting about bits 'n bats of nothing,' said Susan, abstractedly.

'No you weren't. I knocked for ages, you wouldn't be so rude not to open the door,' he replied, quickly.

'Ah yes, but we also went down to the beach, so we must have gone by then,' quipped Dean.

'So you *were* exploring without me!' he uttered, almost bursting into tears on the spot.

'Michael, we are sorry,' said Susan, comforting him. 'We just got carried away chatting, not realising the time, don't get upset, we've not done any exploring yet, honest!'

'Come on,' said Pauline, putting her arm around his shoulders to reassure him. 'Let's go back down to the beach and have a good look around those caves.'

Susan, Dean and Pauline did their best to entertain Michael for the rest of the day, making a fuss of him, knowing full well that if he knew the plans for the night, he'd flip.

The day waned on. It seemed the longest ever. Pauline's hands were moist for most of it, her nervousness setting in. Susan couldn't stop fidgeting. Dean, well he was as cool as ever, talking cryptically to the girls whenever he could about the night's adventure to come.

'Poor Michael,' said Susan, as she entered her room after a late evening meal. 'He's no idea about tonight.'

'S... I'm getting a bit scared,' said Pauline, chewing her lip.

'Oh, we'll be fine,' she said, unconvincingly. Just then, Susan's Mum entered the room after a polite knock.

'Have you entered the talent competition tonight? There's a good prize?'

'Er no, I can't be bothered,' said Susan, again unconvincingly.

'*You* – 'Madam of Drama', aren't taking advantage of an opportunity to shine to the world?' quipped Mrs Watson, in amazement.

'I feel a bit ill,' Susan offered as an excuse.

'I thought you'd been a bit quiet at the dinner table – both of you in fact. How do you feel, Pauline?' asked Mrs Watson, becoming concerned.

'Rather tired,' she yawned, catching onto Susan's thinking.

'Hmm, a bit weak, I just want to lie down,' Susan said, quietly.

'I'll call the doctor,' said Mrs Watson, concerned that both girls felt the same. 'It could be food poisoning,' she pondered. 'Me and your Dad didn't have the chicken, do either of you feel sick?'

'No,' they both chirped, trying to avoid a fuss.

'See how we are in the morning, Mum. I don't think there's any need for a doctor,' Susan said drowsily. 'We've both been running on the beach all day, I think we've done too much. A good night's kip and we'll feel fine.'

'Yeah,' agreed Pauline, with another extended yawn. Duly convinced, Mrs Watson said goodnight.

'Right,' said Susan, switching into first gear, as her Mum closed the door. 'What are we gonna need, do y'think?'

'Will it be warm, do you think we will need a jumper?' asked Pauline, ever practical.

'Yes, we can always take it off.'

'Your Dad's torch?'

'Oh crumbs, I've put it back in their room; I don't think we'll need it.'

'Chocolate?' grinned Pauline.

'Oh defo, at least three bars each!' laughed Susan.

The time marched to 9.55pm. With teddies arranged as before, the girls crept along the corridor and into the secret cupboard as quick as a flash, where Dean was waiting for them. 'Hi, all set for an adventure?' he said, grinning. The girls couldn't smile as easily, the nerves slowly taking over. The lights shone dimly in the old corridor. Maddison suddenly appeared in front of them, beaming with his soft smile, which instantly took away all of their fears.

'Shall we go in the lift?' he suggested, opening the wooden doors. The green lamps created an eerie glow upon Maddison's shiny, fur coat. Nobody spoke, as is often the case in lifts. Tummies turned as the lift descended slowly. Susan looked around the now, familiar wooden box, getting slightly claustrophobic as usual; the light wood panelling was inlaid with leaf patterns on its outer edges. The same rose patterned wallpaper, previously unnoticed here, was perfectly preserved above it. A sharp scented smell made Pauline's nose twitch, which interrupted her made-up vision of the world they were about to enter. Dean retied his shoelaces, ever prepared. The noise of the lift stopped sharply as they reached the basement. The smell of illandrium filled the lift as Maddison opened the doors.

The children all recounted the advice and instructions given by Maddison, with the promise that he would be staying in the lift for the next eleven hours. 'Is your watch set, Dean?' inquired Maddison. 'Don't forget, you must be back before 9am at the latest,' he gently reminded them.

'Don't worry,' said Dean, confidently. 'I'll be checking my watch every half an hour.'

'Where do you think we should head?' said Susan, looking around the darkness of the cave.

'Go and visit my family and ask where Mixy lives,' offered Maddison. 'I'm sure he knows something that will be useful to you.'

Maddison gave a much needed hug to the girls and patted Dean on his shoulders. Cautiously but confidently they followed the daylight out of the cave. As they stepped out, they were amazed at what was before them. Pauline was sure it would be identical to the beach in Marlingham. When it wasn't, they all felt uneasy.

14

NOT WHAT WE THOUGHT

Reaching the entrance of the cave, the air became noticeably chilly. Maddison had informed them that the cave sat in the middle of a little island, which could only be reached by the crossing of a lake. It was probably this geographical fact that had prevented many discovering the secret port way. Although Maddison had told them many things, he had not prepared them for one amazing fact here in Drabacus.

'Wow,' gasped Dean, as he left the cave. 'The lake looks like thick, black treacle.'

'Ooh, it feels eerie, do we have to cross it?' remarked Susan, as she quickly examined her surroundings. Stepping out into the drizzle, something hit them immediately.

'Everything is black and white!' exclaimed Dean. 'There's no colour anywhere.'

'Except on us,' observed Pauline. Each of them felt a little uneasy. The various depths of black and white gave the trees a ghostly form in the distance. The whole place was uninviting, the sky being dark and foreboding. There was something else as well.

'These bushes look withered,' observed Susan, bending down to take a closer look. 'It's as if they've been poisoned.'

'Hmm, they're growing funny as well, aren't they? It's as if they've forgotten what shape they're supposed to be,' Pauline noticed, with her usual eye for detail.

'Come on,' said Dean, with urgency. 'Let's find the boat and oars Maddison has hidden – it's around here somewhere.' After a little searching, Susan spotted an odd shape sticking out of a drooping bush. Not easy, with everything being various shades of grey.

'It's here!' she shouted. Her voice, echoing across the water, disturbed nesting birds in a nearby tree. As they flew close to her head, she was startled, doing a little jump to one side.

'There's mushrooms everywhere,' commented Pauline. 'They don't look like the eating kind, either.' Dean dragged the small boat, letting out a grunt as he did.

'Are the oars in it?'

'Yeah, let's get in. Do you know how to row?' he asked.

'Er no, but we'll pick it up as we go along,' said Susan, confidently. So far, the goal of arriving and finding the boat, had distracted them, but as the boat glided out onto the murky water, fear began to creep up on the girls. Thoughts of bogie men and trolls leapt into mind, the landscaping being the perfect habitat, as it groaned of its neglect.

Unknown to them, they were being observed as they tarried across the water. Attracted by the rainbow of light emanating from the children, small black shapes began to move at the water's edge. 'I'm getting scared,' said Pauline, as she huddled up to Susan, who was busy watching Dean's rowing technique.

'Look,' said Dean, with authority in his voice. 'Remember what Maddison told us. That no matter how strange things appear, we are always safe and not far from home.' And so, entrusted with this thought in their hearts and minds, they continued to the other side, feeling stronger.

The journey only took four minutes, although it felt much longer. The wind had discovered them out in the open, and had begun to flick Susan's fringe into her eyes. It wasn't cold, but it was wet, as the wind brought light spots of rain, which was slowly beginning to soak them through.

'We'd better hide the boat for later,' said Dean, as they all climbed out.

Looking back to the island, all that could be distinguished of the cave was a dark grey mound, which merged into its background. They tried to lock the monotonous image into their memories for their return, discussing which bits each would remember. The grey surroundings made everything look blank, and it was extremely difficult finding anything to identify at all. At least they wouldn't lose each other, being flushed with colour, they stood out like hundreds and thousands on soft ice cream.

Dean had decided to wear his bottle green jumper and bright blue trousers, whilst Susan and Pauline had opted for multi-coloured T-shirts underneath red and yellow cardigans and blue jeans which half covered blue 'Jesus' sandals, all the latest teenage fashion. Colourful slides adorned their hair, and an aura of brightness shone from them.

They moved through a small copse of trees, which overhung in a sorrowful state. Beyond this was a wide path made of fallen bark. The sky was still grey, but now they saw brightness overhead, which instinctively told them it wasn't night time, but just a dull day. All of a sudden, several birds accompanied them from the trees nearby. Flying low, and swapping branches, they seemed to be following them. The colourful trio attracted more of them as they made their way down the path, which was distinguishable only by the texture and noise of crunching beneath their feet. Pauline's blue sandals had become extra shiny in the wet, and everyone's clothes now had a covering of fine, tiny raindrops. The water slowly dripped from everyone's hair, tickling their noses as it did. The track started to descend into a small valley. In its midst, sat a small row of houses.

'Now, Maddison's family must live here,' said Dean, as his pace quickened down the hill.

'Hmm, these houses seem to be the only ones around,' said Susan, as she squinted to see anything else hiding in the greyness.

'Shall we knock on a few doors and ask?' Pauline enquired confidently, as she hunched the red bag of goodies she'd brought, over her shoulder. The children noticed that animals had also begun to join the birds following them. Two large rabbits and a small, wild deer, were all captivated by the dazzling hues of colour which shone out from the visitors amongst the grey, bleached out conditions. On closer inspection, the houses looked like they were made from fondant icing sugar, having a smooth, round appearance.

'Hmm, they look like they've been made in a cookery class, the walls seem to glisten like yummy icing on a birthday cake,' said Pauline, starting to feel hungry.

'Hmm, and the roof looks like a gigantic Walnut Whip with cream spilling out of the top.' Susan's thoughts obviously focused on chocolate. 'That reminds me, Peewee, get me one out will you.'

Dean walked up a two-tone grey path, which perfectly matched the doorway and surround. His shoe studs clipping loudly, announcing his arrival. Giving a loud knock, he stepped back, to be joined by the girls who had decided to delay the eating of chocolate for a minute. Several more knocks produced no reply. It was the same at the five other houses.

A little voice, unfamiliar in tone, then interrupted. Looking around, to their amazement, it was one of the rabbits. 'No-one ever answers the door,' it said, shyly.

After their initial shock, cushioned a little by hearing Maddison speak, Dean asked, 'Why not?'

'Well, everyone stays in bed usually. There's not a lot to get up for, except for their food.'

'What, everyone?' he asked, disbelievingly.

'Pretty much,' replied the other rabbit, which had really big, floppy ears.

'We usually stay indoors too, but we heard all the birds singing so loudly today, we thought we'd take a look at what was going on.'

'Where are you from?' said the little deer, moving forwards as she gained confidence. 'You are beautiful.'

'Oh, you mean the colour,' responded Susan. 'Have you never seen it before?'

'No, I don't think so – I can't remember,' replied the fawn, who had white spots all over her neck of grey. Her black hooves looked like walking boots.

'It's wonderful to see such a sight,' said the second rabbit.

'A real tonic. My cold seems much better, just for seeing you,' commented the first rabbit that had spoken. The birds continued their flights of fancy, fluttering up and down in obvious delight at the children's arrival.

'Do you know where Maddison's family, the monkeys live?' asked Dean, quite excited at all the attention they were attracting.

'Maddison! You know Maddison?' they all gasped.

'Yes, he's sent us on a little mission,' replied Pauline, pleased at being associated with someone they all knew and loved. The little deer quickly beckoned the three to follow her, introducing herself as Frilly. The children explained their goals to the animals along the way, but the only information that Frilly could help with was the way to Maddison's family. As they chatted, the animals were clearly unaware of anything else that had gone on in Drabacus.

In front of them soon appeared another cave. Several monkeys approached the children, immediately attracted by their colourful presence. They somehow knew that Maddison had sent the children for some reason.

15

THE AWAKENINGS BEGIN

The excitement was infectious, bringing all the monkeys out of an apparent hibernation. Around them stood several large trees with sweeping branches, which made obvious napping posts. About eight family members gathered.

'It feels so good to have you around,' said a kindly monkey, with a band of jet-black fur around her neck, hanging as a scarf would. 'Whenever Maddison has come to see us, and it's not been very often, we are all awakened with sheer joy for a short while, and he is full of colour as you are, but the feeling doesn't last.'

'Take a seat,' said Jobim, one of the elder monkeys, who just looked like an older Maddison, but he was monotone. 'How can we help you?' he asked, as he passed around banana-shaped objects, indicating they were to be eaten. Dean explained the story clearly, expressing urgency at the deadline. Already three quarters of an hour had passed by his watch.

'Well,' said Dean, drawing in breath quickly, 'Maddison said you know where we could find a man called Mixy Lune?'

'Yes, does he live here?' interrupted Susan.

'Hmm, Mixy,' pondered Jobim. 'He lives in the big house at the end of the village, but he's not very well.'

'Oh blimey, that's all we need,' said Dean, pulling a face.

'Aw, what's the matter with him?' said Pauline, more sympathetically.

'He's not himself,' said the monkey with the lookalike scarf, who was called Meedo. 'You cannot tell what he's saying, he gets mixed up a lot which is why he's now called Mixy. In fact, I've just remembered!' she exclaimed, jumping wildly about with excitement. 'He's really called Maximillian!'

'Oh yes,' said Jobim, starting to jump around with glee. 'That's right, and he used to be the Mayor of Abacus, it's all coming back to me now,' he exclaimed.

Somehow, the children's brightness had caused the renewal of memory to the surrounding animals. Just like when you add cooling coals back to a red-hot fire, they start to burn brightly once more. The animals basked in the joy and warmth of the visitors, and began to awaken slowly to their plight of being stuck in a dreary existence. Dean quickly informed the monkeys about the missing key and Erasmus Drab's involvement.

'Where is Drab's castle?' asked Pauline, as she looked about the non-descript landscape.

'There's a map about somewhere,' said Meedo. 'It's at the back of the cave I think.' And off she popped to get it. She was back in a jiffy, looking really pleased with herself.

The map was extremely old, on paper as thin as tissue. It tore slightly as Dean began to open it. Drabacus was not a big place, covering approximately a perfect square mile, giving rise to its original name, Abacus. The castle sat in the south-east corner, about three thousand steps through the trees from their present position. In fact, the lake they had crossed, sat dead centre. The landscape appeared very hilly in the north, with a much larger lake in the north-west corner.

'You are very lucky that I've been able to find it, Erasmus Drab ordained that every piece of writing paper and writing implement was to be destroyed, in the Order of the Riva, many moons ago.'

'What do you mean, ordained?' asked Susan, ever asking questions.

'It means it became a rule,' Jobim told her.

'Why?' asked all three, quizzically.

'That bit I cannot remember,' said Jobim, looking puzzled again.

'No, neither can I,' said Meedo, equally confused, 'but I remember at the time it seemed a good idea. We do not need to write things down and I think that's why we didn't really bother about it.'

'Do you not write stories or poems?' asked Pauline. The monkeys shook their heads.

Right,' said Dean, with gusto. 'We need to be going.'

'Yes,' said Pauline, 'we've a lot to do yet,' gathering up her red bag.

'Why don't you go and see Maddison?' suggested Susan to the monkeys. 'The doorway is open now and he's in the cave waiting for our return.'

'What a splendid idea,' they agreed, jumping up and down in unison at the news. Dean explained where to find the boat, and they said their goodbyes for now.

Tucking the map into his trouser pocket, they set off to Mixy's house, accompanied still by Frilly and the two rabbits, called Bosun and Leo. The whole area, grey and uninteresting, cast a dull haze over the land, making everything mingle together. Frilly had kindly agreed to guide them.

'You can hardly pick anything out,' said Susan, trying to focus on a broken piece of stone one of the following birds had rested on. 'Was this a milestone or a signpost at one time?' Susan asked of the grey pillar, with its sharp triangle edge sticking upwards, out of the withered grass.

'Hmm,' pondered Frilly. 'I think there was some kind of script on it at one time. It got broken by Drab personally, when the Order of the Riva came.'

'Whatever it was, it was important to Drab, when things changed,' said Dean, excitedly. 'Let's get a better look.'

'I think the act, that stopped all writing, was significant in his plans,' said Susan, 'I mean, without being able to read or write things, that would definitely block and rob someone of their creativity. I don't know what I'd do without being able to write my diary every day,' said Susan, disturbed at the thought.

'Me too, S,' agreed Pauline.

'Don't do diaries,' said Dean, shaking his head with a smirk, 'but I get what you mean.'

The stone, now about two feet in height, was well weathered with the dreary, damp conditions. A covering of lichen crept up its sides. It felt spongy on top where moss seedlings had sprouted in a wonderful shade of grey. Searching around the sides at the top, Pauline could feel some indentations. She peeled back the moss, which on closer inspection revealed some kinds of markings, unknown in origin to the three foreigners.

'What does this say?' asked Dean to the three animals.

'I don't know,' they each replied, disappointingly.

Frilly explained further, 'We animals have no need to read and write. We rely on people to tell us what we need to know. Mixy may know more,' she offered.

It wasn't like any kind of writing the children had ever seen before. Looking more like Egyptian hieroglyphics, but nowhere near as complicated.

'I'll copy this down in my note pad,' said Dean, 'it may be useful in the future.'

'Hark at you,' noted Susan, annoyed that she hadn't thought to bring a pen and notebook.

Onward they travelled, passing by the houses they'd called at earlier. There was still no sign of life.

16

MIXY'S MOMENT

They trundled on until they reached the last house in the cluster. This home certainly felt as if the owner had left long ago. What looked like rubbish was strewn down either side of the path, the grey grass had grown long and uneven, with large patches of moss dotted all over. Frilly and the rabbits stayed in the untidy garden, nibbling at the grass, whilst the children attempted to gain a reply at the unloved house. The letters M L on the door gave the only clue as to its occupant. After many determined knocks, a bit of mumbling and clattering could be heard from inside. A shuffle clearly indicated that someone was up and about to answer the door. The children became momentarily nervous for a few seconds, before a tall, portly man opened it.

'Er, wrong something?' he asked, his eyes screwing up in puzzlement.

'Are you Mixy Lune?' asked Dean in a forthright manner, noticing immediately that his dark, grey hair was long, scraggly and hanging off his shoulder.

'By murd!' exclaimed Mixy Lune, as he sprang back, the colour hitting the back of his eyeballs. 'My woodness, I tidnot dink colour still exsisted many bore, it is lo song I have seen any since.' He flabbergasted. Although it seemed a bit rude, the children couldn't help but giggle at the obvious bungling of his words. Mixy Lune became so excited that he tried to ask three questions, all at the same time, completely failing to make himself be understood by anyone.

'Slow down,' said Susan laughing gently, trying to calm him.

'Now,' said Dean, with a gentler tone in his voice, 'I'll tell you why we are here while you get your breath back.'

Mixy Lune repeated the grey and uninteresting theme of his world. His clothes reminded Pauline of a cheery gnome she had in her garden. These consisted of simple trousers, tied with string at the waist, and a tunic with wooden buttons, which hung over a ruffled shirt. His face however was lovely and rounded. He had begun to beam as the wave of colour washed over his tired spirit, revealing a beautiful broad, white smile. He was really rather a handsome fellow. He welcomed them inside the untidy cottage. As he led them in, they noticed the rest of his hair was tied in a ponytail, hanging half way down his back.

They entered one large room. He began to light a fire to warm them, using lots of dried grass just scattered on the wooden floor. All three children felt like picking it up, it looked so cluttered, but it seemed rather rude, so they offered to make a drink instead, as they were all feeling thirsty, not to mention tired. It was of course, way past their bedtime. Dean preferred to help Mixy roll the grass into firm balls, to make lighting the fire easier. Another scouting skill coming in handy.

'He hasn't tidied up in years!' uttered Pauline under her breath, as she looked at the sink full of grime as they entered the kitchen. 'My Mum would go bananas if I left my room like this – he's a grown man.'

'Yeah, but he's got problems, hasn't he?' offered Susan, in defence. 'He probably doesn't even know what day of the week it is, or even care.'

'I wonder if they have Monday and Tuesday here?' Pauline thought aloud.

'Well, I don't suppose he has any tea,' she commented to Pauline. 'What shall we drink, Mixy?' she asked, popping her head around the doorframe.

'Oer, look in that bottle grey shelf end of.' Despite all the bottles being grey, Susan had a peep in several and chose one. Sniffing it, she decided that it would be ok to drink, smelling a bit like water with lemon in it.

Dean had been busy explaining everything to Mixy in the meantime, and he had calmed down. He had almost stopped getting his words back to front. A few rogue ones crept in here and there, but Dean was able to understand him much better. Again, the brightness of Mixy's visitors had a very positive effect on him, restoring his memory and helping him regain many thoughts, long hidden away. The fire was now roaring and the girls decided to share out some chocolate along with the drinks.

'So, what do you remember from the past?' asked Pauline, as she bit into her Twix.

'Oh the past, the past, let me recall…what can I now remember?' he pondered, with his head in his hands. Mixy acted as if he was waking from a hundred year sleep. 'It seems so long ago that something *different* happened,' he said slowly, but surely. 'Each day has been the same since…well, forever now.'

'Try Mixy!' said Susan, with urgency in her voice. 'We need you to remember so we can find our stolen key. Can you remember anything about that?' Pauline and Dean started to throw in suggestions about what it could have been like.

'Was it ever sunny?'

'Did it rain?'

'Was everything colour like us?'

'Do you remember the key?'

Mixy's brain started to compute. 'Key, key, key,' he said, aloud. 'Drob drapped it!' he suddenly exclaimed.

'You mean Drab dropped it,' corrected Dean, with a smile. 'Yes, we know that, do you know where He took it?'

'Not for sure, but it will be at the citadel,' he answered.

'So, it's in the south east corner, as we saw on the map,' said Susan.

'Yes, just beyond the main town, you will not miss it.'

'Is it guarded?' asked Dean.

'Guarded!' exclaimed Mixy, 'why would anyone want to guard it? No-one wants to go there!'

'Why?' said Pauline, nervously.

'Because we do not live there!' said Mixy, puzzled that anyone would want to go visiting Drab. 'No,' said Mixy, matter of factly, 'we all just keep ourselves to ourselves. I just go out for something to eat each day. Erasmus Drab provides all that for free.'

'For free, why?' said Dean, immediately suspicious. 'No-one does anything for free, is there no food that you can buy or grow for yourselves?'

'Why would we want to do that?' asked Mixy, taking a sip of his lemon drink. 'I cannot see the point of that.'

'Do you ever have parties on your birthday?' asked Pauline, finishing her first bar of Twix. Susan interrupted his reply.

'Mixy, you've not eaten your chocolate, try some, it's really good,' said Susan coaxingly, pointing to the untouched piece.

'Is it safe to eat?' he asked, cautiously. 'That's why we eat Erasmus Drab's food, safe we know it is.'

'Why, has everything been poisoned?' asked Dean, suddenly sitting up straight.

'Well, Erasmus Drab says we cannot be sure about anything else, so we only eat and drink what He provides. Last time someone tried anything else, they became ill.'

'Sounds like a classic case of brain-washing to me,' commented Dean to the girls.

'What's that?' asked Susan, as usual.

'It's a form of mind control, where you are made to believe certain things that may be true or untrue. You can't tell. It can make you falsely dependent on people.'

'Oh right, I see, said the blind man,' said Susan, quoting one of her favourite sayings when things became clear. 'Come on Mixy, try it, we practically live on it!' gestured Susan. Mixy slowly picked up the bar, sniffing it first. The smell of chocolate went flying up his nostrils.

'Why murd!' he exclaimed, and quickly chomped off a big piece. 'Hmm, ohh,' his tongue squirmed at the exquisite taste, exploding like fireworks on every taste bud in his mouth. He nearly fell off his chair as he swooned in sheer delight at the chocolate melting and sliding around his mouth. It was just too good to swallow yet, so he hung on to it, letting the biscuit crunch on his tongue. Susan, Dean and Pauline laughed at Mixy's new experience of chocolate. It seemed to liven him up somewhat. Finally, when Mixy did swallow the piece of chocolate biscuit, he bumbled five sentences all at once, trying to describe the taste sensation. Pauline worked out that, overall, he thoroughly enjoyed the lot and could he please have some more!

'If you tell us something else,' teased Susan waving around the wrapping paper in front of his nose.

'Oh my,' said Mixy, as he recovered. He had really perked up after the chocolate treat. 'It's such a long time since I've tasted anything so marvellous.'

'Why, what does Drab give you?' asked Pauline.

'This,' he said, as he went to fetch a round, grey bowl, which looked like a teapot without a spout. Peeking inside, the children pulled up their noses at the contents, which resembled old porridge that had been made too lumpy. 'It's good,' said Mixy, trying to convince himself.

'You think it's good because you don't know anything else!' exclaimed Dean. 'That's awful, what else do you have?'

'That is it, I have the same every day. Compared to the chocolate, it IS very bland I suppose, but I've just got used to it,' said Mixy, now realising what a boring diet he was really being given. Susan broke off another piece of chocolate and gave it to him. His eyes lit up at what he now knew he was going to experience.

Dean pulled out the markings he had made in his notebook. 'Do you know what these are?' he said, holding them up to Mixy's face.

'Sheeboo, natilliate, bebondeo!' exclaimed Mixy. Not one of the children understood a word he said. Suddenly, Mixy started jumping around the room, flinging his arms around, shouting and clapping. 'The Sanguine, The Sanguine,' he sang at the top of his voice. He started to hum something, but he just couldn't get it right. He was obviously very excited, even more so than the effect of the chocolate. 'You have sound fumthing, have you got the rest?' he said, with a big grin. 'Oh, I have not felt like this since, oh well, I can't think, but you have made me remember something I had forgotten.'

'What?' said the trio, now getting equally excited.

'How to be happy,' he cheered, and promptly danced around the room. The children couldn't help but join in his merriment. It was infectious in this dreary room of grey. It seemed that all Mixy needed was to rub shoulders, so to speak, with other people who were not weighed down with hopelessness and a lack of interest or concern about others. The combination of the children's brightness, the new taste of chocolate and the script that Dean had shown to him, revitalised Mixy to such a degree, that his brain released all his good memories which had been trapped, so that power and joy flowed back into his life. They came rushing in like a flood, which he began to tell with great effect.

'Erasmus Drab arrived suddenly, many eons ago. At first, His appearance in Abacus seemed unimportant, everybody going about his or her business as usual. Everything was colourful, as you three are, and we all regularly met to sing and eat together. We would grow our own food in the fields beyond the lake,' he paused to recall it all. 'We all helped each other, everyone did something to get the job done, and we worked as a team to ease the load. My job was to see that things were done at the right time. Others would plant the seed, some watered every day, and so on.

'Then, out of the blue, someone announced that they thought they were working harder than others, and wanted to do less. Erasmus Drab had spent a lot of time with this person. Rumours started to spread that the food was bad for you anyway. The people that had complained started to stay away from our regular get-togethers, so friendships started to break down and bad feelings set in. At the same time though, no-one thought to sort it all out, and we all started keeping ourselves to ourselves. Not getting together as we once had.

'I remember that Erasmus Drab suggested a solution. HE would kindly provide our food to stop any arguments, and ensure the food was safe to eat. This seemed to be the best solution at the time. Once people began to trust Erasmus

Drab, He then suggested that He knew what was best for us all, and gave us the Order of the Riva, which banned all writing in the land. This included getting rid of our quills, and everything that was written. This, we were told, would get rid of all the nasty letters, which folk had started to receive anonymously.

'No-one I knew had got one, but we all agreed that this would be a good solution to the problem. Since then, everyone has felt rather low, nothing to get excited about. The same dreary day, every day, forever. No-one feels any urge to change things. We are all content the way we are.'

'You're not content Mixy,' blurted out Dean, angrily. 'You've been kept away from anything worth hoping for, robbed of your worthiness, tricked into thinking you're a nobody, that you don't matter or make a difference to anyone or anything.'

'In short, you've stopped believing in yourself,' announced Susan, equally annoyed at all that Mixy had shared.

'I think you're right,' spluttered Mixy. 'I have never felt so alive and excited. I… I… I used to be Mayor, you know,' he beamed with pride.

'Oh Mixy,' said Susan, gleefully, 'I'm so glad you've remembered, now keep these good thoughts in your mind, eh.'

'Yep, think positive, that's what my brother, Steven, is always saying,' said Pauline, with a finger pointing in the air.

'What's on this shelf, Mixy?' asked Susan, curiously. She was especially known for her nosiness, each year always finding well-hidden Christmas presents. Not that she ever let on, mind.

'Ooer that, now,' he paused. 'Let me think, er, it's been there for ages,' he pondered slowly, trying his best to remember. 'Oh yes,' he said, with wonder and mystery in his voice. 'That young girl that visited Abacus on the trail of Drab, as you call Him, lost it on her visit. She was so excited at what Erasmus Drab dropped on the floor, that she did not notice her pretty little circle slipping off her arm. So I picked it up and placed it on that shelf, in case she ever came back. But she never did, and soon I forgot all about it in all my dreariness. It's a wonder it's still here. I have seen it loads of times, but could not quite remember what it was doing there.'

Susan picked up the delicate, silver-looking Victorian bracelet, and with a clip of a clasp, she admired it glinting on her own arm. In an instant, it turned gold, as it was restored on Susan's arm.

Suddenly, the sound of trumpets and horses' hooves could be heard in the distance. Mixy jumped from his seat. 'Erasmus Drab's daily procession,' he said, with dread in his voice. 'I have to go and get today's food ration.'

'You're on rations!' said Dean, disbelievingly.

'Blimey,' commented Pauline, with a moan, 'I couldn't be doing with that,' as she stuffed the last bit of Twix into her mouth.

'Come along with me,' said Mixy quickly, and with fear in his voice. 'If I'm not there on time, I will miss out.'

'Flippin' heck, he's got you in a right old boring, daily routine,' said Pauline.

'Hasn't he?' nodded Susan.

'If it's like the food you've just shown us, I wouldn't worry if I were you!' said Dean, with a smile.

17

THE GAME STARTS

They trundled out one by one, in crocodile fashion. It was apparent that some kind of procession was taking place in the distant streets of the town.

'We have to wait at a certain place,' said Mixy, matter of factly.

'Rules, flippin' rules,' cried Pauline. 'Why can't you just go to a shop at a time to suit you?'

'I suppose now I think about it, He likes to remind everyone how kind He is,' answered Mixy.

'Huh, well I don't see that,' said Dean. 'He's just got you all hoodwinked.'

'But it is free,' Mixy reminded him.

'You couldn't charge for that muck you showed me,' retorted Dean, raising a smile from the girls.

'Hmm, I suppose I have teen baken in quite a bit, without realising it,' said Mixy, getting his words about turn again.

The sky was grey and dark clouds seemed to follow the procession, which was crawling nearer, as if some impending doom was about to make itself known. As the three visitors looked on, they didn't notice that everyone else who had come out for their food, was now looking at them, attracted to the flash of bright colour flowing out from their clothes. Mixy noticed this and advised the three to hide behind the crowds, if they could, as not to draw attention to themselves. It was impossible though, to hide the blaze of colour streaming from them. The noise of talking, unheard by Mixy for many years, began to fill the streets, as people stared and were being moved by the children's presence, instead of standing in an orderly line to be fed by the approaching food givers.

The children in turn were made motionless, by the extremely large, black carriage, like ones that would have been seen in a time long ago, before any car had even been dreamt of. It sat in the middle of four gigantic, wrought iron wheels, supported by polished blade-like spokes, which flashed as they turned. Its six windows were blackened out to hide the occupants. The whole thing had to be pulled along by six black, stallion horses, with sinister smiles. The children started to shake as it approached them. He who was inside, had indeed noticed that today, the town's folk were acting differently. Where was His order? What were His obedient and grateful subjects discussing, that He did not know about? He leaned to the window.

The children stood out like drops of blood on snow. He gasped with delight. Erasmus Drab smirked at the plan He was now conjuring up, and became excited that the doorway was obviously open again. For years, He had dreamed of returning to the vast crowds of people for whom He would become Master. But that doorway had eluded Him.

Behind the carriage, people raised their hands for the daily supply of bread and gruel. Well, that's honestly what it was. It was handed out by what could only be described as deformed garden gnomes, each dressed as if from a time where fashion hadn't been invented. Everything, strangely triangular. Hats, flags and shoes, rather like those of court jesters. Everyone held out his or her pots to be filled. A little man on a large cart, following behind Erasmus Drab's carriage, was pouring gruel in the pots as he passed by. Another little man thrust a piece of bread, which looked like it had forgotten how to rise evenly whilst in the oven, into the other free hand. Drab had them begging, and they didn't even notice. 'This is safe to eat,' he droned to each person in the line, as the tasteless meals were given out.

Susan, Dean and Pauline had tried to keep well behind the line of town's folk, but He had seen them. Well, you couldn't miss them. The children were rooted to the spot as they looked at the shadowy windows, obscuring its occupant, moving ever nearer.

Then, as if by magic, Erasmus Drab's face appeared, as if someone had taken out the darkened glass. What they saw surprised them. For in the carriage sat one of the most handsome young men any of them had ever seen. He had bouncing black, curly locks of hair, falling about His shoulders. His dazzling eyes shone like jewels, complemented by full black lashes you would see in a mascara advert. A perfectly formed nose and lips finished off His model-like face. He was certainly very elegant. Susan and Pauline immediately compared him to Donny Osmond and David Cassidy, their current pop singer heroes.

The children, standing out as obvious aliens in this dreary world of grey then heard these words, loudly delivered by Erasmus Drab in a chilled, calm voice, as He slowed down the carriage. 'Oh, we have visitors I see, I almost missed you,' He remarked, unnerved. 'You must be feeling at home here, you are already beginning to fade,' He pointed. 'You'll soon fit in nicely,' He laughed. The window of the carriage was darkened once more, and off He went, acting like a King on a royal tour. His words stabbed at Pauline, her face turning paler at his patter. Susan immediately yawned, the tiredness catching up on her. Dean turned to them.

'The cheek of that man, did you hear Him, 'fit in nicely' indeed!' sneered Dean, in disgust.

'What did He mean?' You are already beginning to fade,' puzzled Pauline.

'Oh, He was nice-looking though,' said Susan, almost swooning after the encounter. 'Although, there was something unusual about His face and I can't think what.'

'Never mind He's nice looking! The guy's a thief,' Dean reminded them. 'And He's probably got our key hidden in his castle, come on, let's follow that carriage.'

'Is that your plan?' asked Mixy, cautiously. 'He will know you are following Him. He always goes back to the citadel after His rounds, so just hold back a bit. I will take you to the moat house.'

'Do you know,' declared Pauline, 'You two do look a little paler…less bright, I've only just noticed it since Drab pointed it out.'

'Oh,' said Susan, with a further yawn, 'you don't look any different to me.'

'Well, I don't suppose it matters that much,' said Pauline, copying Susan's infectious yawn.

'Mixy, onwards to the moat house,' commanded Dean.

The skies of Drabacus were now getting lighter as it became midday. The rain had stopped some time ago, although no-one noticed because they had all got used to the fine drizzle. Folks gradually stopped staring as they passed through the humdrum streets, everyone making their way back home, the day's drama over once more, all to be repeated again tomorrow.

Along the way were a couple of shops, which appeared to be empty of people. The door frames were made of polished steel, and they looked very posh indeed. There was no buzz about visiting the shops, like back home though. No excitement about the place at all. Susan and Pauline couldn't wait for Saturday mornings, when they would travel with their Mums to the big town, to browse and spend their hard-earned spends. Shopping is fun! But here, there didn't seem to be anything worth having in these shops. The girls entered one, seeing souvenir gifts of Drab's castle, ornaments of Erasmus Drab in various regal poses, and artificial flowers, in a choice of black and white. Not a bag of toffees in sight.

'You wouldn't need any spending money here,' commented Pauline, as she scanned the store, looking for something interesting.

'That's a nice picture of Erasmus Drab,' replied Susan, unexpectedly. 'I think my Mum would approve of that one on the wall.' Dean joined them, having spotted a fine scale model of Drab's horses and carriage in the window.

'That would go quite nicely with my karting trophies. Look at the detail in that horse's face.'

'Do we want souvenirs of Drabacus?' asked Pauline.

'I think I'd like something to remind me of my visit,' replied Susan, getting rather attached to the picture she had seen.

'How much is stuff?' Pauline asked Mixy, with a yawn.

'Well, since no-one works anymore, no-one has any credits. Drab provides all the furniture for our homes, but I've never wanted anything, I can't see the need.'

'You mean everything's free!' said Susan, who never missed a bargain.

'Hey great, 'yawned Dean, 'we'll pick some up on the way back if we've time, eh.'. Pauline picked up a silver oval frame It was a signed picture of Drab in a super cool pose.

'I'll have this now, it's not too big, it will fit in my bag,' said Pauline, frightened it would go before she returned.

'I'd like to see in the other shop,' said Susan, spotting the flower shop across the path. 'Look at these P, aren't they unusual? I've never seen mushrooms look so peculiar, but they do look nice.'

'That's a deadly nightshade,' said Dean. 'I can tell with its umbrella-shaped top. If it were in colour, it would be red with white spots.'

'I think these other plants are tropical, they're so huge,' said Susan, now overshadowed by six large leaves.

'That's an Amazonian orchid,' remarked Dean. 'I can tell by its big tongue sticking out, it would be red too.'

'Who are you?' said Pauline, sarcastically. 'Nephew of David Attenborough?'

'He's just showing off, as usual,' Susan retorted. 'Anyway, I think it's a big lily. I've seen some like it on a trip to Kew Gardens, last summer,' she said with another yawn, immediately copied by Pauline and Dean.

'Can we not have a short kip, Dean?' asked Susan, with a little moan in her voice.

'Ooh yeah,' responded Pauline, immediately. 'I'm pooped!'

'It won't do us any harm, I guess,' said Dean, who had clearly taken charge of the expedition. 'Mixy, where can we go for a lie down?'

'There's a hodging louse on the way, you can stop off there,' he mumbled.

'Did you mean lodging house, Mixy?' laughed Dean.

'Yes, it's Drab's Erasmotel,' he replied.

'Mixy, you're getting worse, but I can understand you, just about!' yawned Dean one more time.

As they turned the corner, the lodging house stood out like a black tooth in a perfect set of pearly white teeth. Its appearance on the outside was like shiny black Lego blocks, neatly fitted together with a glass, triangular roof. Inside, although it was black and white, it was quite exquisite in its décor, having ornate lamps, soft to the touch rugs and large wall coverings in its entrance hall.

'Wow, this is nice,' announced Pauline, admiring all the intricate ornaments and trinkets by the huge fireplace. Above it, a large sign displayed the welcoming words,

LODGE FREE AND REST YOUR BONES A WHILE

Courtesy of Erasmus Drab, your kindly host.

'That's nice of Him,' said Pauline, surprisingly. 'To provide accommodation for anyone passing, free of charge. I mean. It's lovely here. Look at this fluffy chair, it's all the rage at home.'

'Hmm, He doesn't seem to be as bad as we've been made to think,' agreed Susan.

'Remember, He pinched the key, and that's a fact that Maddison gave us,' Dean reminded both of them.

'Yes, but did He? Maddison's only going off what young Ada *thought* she saw,' Susan suggested, with another yawn.

'But, we've held a piece of the key that Drab dropped!' said Dean, frustrated at Susan's sudden ability to forget all the facts so easily. Mixy, noticing that all three were extremely tired, due to the increasing arguments, suggested that they all took advantage of a good rest, rather than a quick kip.

'I'll set my watch to beep in two of our hours,' said Dean. 'it still gives us seven hours once we wake up, I'm sure we'll all feel much better after a little sleep.' Dean headed towards a small chap with a pointed hat and big ears on the reception desk. Mixy agreed a time to come back, and left. The Receptionist suggested that to get the best rest, they should have a room each. They didn't argue about that, and headed off to what seemed like paradise.

'Ah, just to get my head on a pillow and sleep,' cried Pauline, as she entered her room to see a large bed beckon her eyes, with the fluffiest cushions and shiny, silk sheets. Sleep overtook the weary travellers in an instant.

Elsewhere, inside the Erasmotel, the Receptionist nodded as he took instructions from Drab.

18

OBLIVIOUS

Outside, the sky became very dark, as the Drabacus evening began to roll in quickly. Any stray folks returned to their homes to light fires and have a meal. While the children slept through two of their hours, Drabacus passed through the night and half of the following morning. The grey clouds were covering the three suns of Drabacus. Mixy knew he had said he'd be at the Erasmotel at some time during this day, but couldn't quite remember why. Frilly had to remind him, as she came to his door to travel with him, as arranged the previous day.

Dean was busy in a sword fight with a tall, dark stranger, when the intermittent buzz of his watch started to distract his concentration, and the stranger caught him off guard, and injured his left arm. Thankfully, the pain that had begun to hurt in his dream, disappeared as he began to wake in his black and white room. Two hours was clearly not enough time to sweep away the tiredness he was now faced with, feeling seven times worse than before his head had hit the pillow. In his judgement, another couple of hours would be fine, and he promptly set his watch to buzz again at 4am Marlingham time. It only took seconds to drift off again, to challenge the stranger once more. He'd no sooner returned to fight his opponent, then the alarm came again. He hadn't even drawn his sword. There must be something wrong with his watch he mumbled in a daze, and promptly squeezed the button to shut it off completely.

Meanwhile, poor Mixy and Frilly, were trying to gain entry into the Erasmotel. It was way past the time the children had agreed to meet him, Drabacus having passed through another day and night. The doors to the shiny, brick lodging house were firmly shut, and there was nothing Mixy and Frilly could do to stir the three travellers from their deep, and much needed sleep.

'Oh dear,' moaned Mixy.

'Yes?' said Frilly, thinking Mixy wanted her.

'I'm at a loss to know what I'm doing here,' he puzzled. 'I've to collect my daily food allowance any minute now. Frilly, will you stay here and see if anybody appears, or dopens the oars and come and tell me if they do? I'm sure it will bum sack to me, eventually.'

'Of course,' she offered, gently. 'Now run along, or you'll be late.'

Back at the Erasmotel, all was quiet inside. Flies didn't dare buzz. The children didn't know it, but precious time was ebbing away as they dreamed on of fights, chocolate, keys and caramel castles. It was Susan who stirred first and this was very unusual, she was the deepest sleeper ever. She once slept through a house fire across the road in her street. She was most annoyed with her Mum for not waking her up, as all the neighbours had been out and about in an array of rollered hair and pink dressing gowns, to see the two fire engines and five fire fighters taking two hours to put it out. The man had only wakened because his dog had barked at him, and he escaped out of the window, and had run down the street in the nude. That was the real reason she had been annoyed. Everyone was talking about the sight of the poor man running around with no clothes on, his dog barking after him, for weeks.

Susan hadn't closed the grey-striped curtains, and it was light bouncing off her eyelids that had disturbed her sleep. She never bothered with a watch, uncannily always knowing the time of day. It was often due to the position of the sun, combined with the last known time. She was pretty good at it too, always being within five minutes of the right time. Here however, there was no sun to be seen, not that it may even rise in the east and set in the west, as it did back home. And the last known time? Well, she had been so tired, she didn't even bother to listen to what Dean had said. So, as she awoke in her room of black and white, she not only didn't know what time of day it was, but also wondered where the heck she was. Eventually, the room gave itself away.

'Oh yes,' she thought aloud. 'Now I'm feeling much better for a rest. I'm in Drabacus on a mission.' Feeling very relaxed, she sat up and crouched on the end of the bed with her head on her knees, hands firmly clasped around her bunched up legs. She was trying to think of things, but she just couldn't progress her thoughts any further than feeling thirsty, and looked around for something to drink. What was the mission? she kept saying to herself over and over again. Spotting a glass, with what looked like blackcurrant in it on the table by the window, she slowly uncurled herself with a big stretch and a yawn. She moved over to it and unguarded, began to quench her thirst.

Outside, she noted the grey sky along with all the trees, people and paths. Once you had seen it all in grey for a while, you actually got used to it, all fitting in quite nicely, quite normal really. As she spotted a Walnut Whip sticking out of her sling bag, it reminded her that Pauline was in the room next door and Big Head was just across the hall. Susan made her way to Pauline's room. Her hair needed brushing, sticking out all over the place, but good grooming had never been her first priority, and she hadn't thought to bring a comb. Remembering how nice Erasmus was as she passed by His picture in the hallway, she hoped Pauline had brought one. Susan gave three, loud knocks to her door. Pauline was never good at getting up in the morning, always the last one to rise, then blaming everyone else for not waking her up in time, when she was late for school. Susan tried the handle. It opened. Pauline wasn't good at security either!

Still in a deep sleep, Pauline lay on her tummy, fully clothed, as she had fallen asleep earlier. Lying on her left cheek forced her mouth to gape open in an 'O' shape. She looked comical. Susan started to shake her long-time friend. 'Pauline, wake up,' she started off, in a sort of whisper, only to go on to loud shouts. After five attempts, life appeared, and Pauline opened her right eye, the left one being squashed into the pillow. 'Ungh,' she grunted, in a sleepy daze. The sight of Susan five inches away from her nose, looking like a hair bear, soon made her get a grip. 'Oh,' she moaned, 'time to get up already?'

Well, I don't know, the army sergeant hasn't appeared for line-up duty yet,' quipped Susan sarcastically of Dean. Pauline laughed. He was rather bossy. Sitting up on the bed, Pauline slowly came around. 'Have you got a comb or something?' Susan anxiously asked of Pauline.

'Er, I think so,' she said, leaning over to her bag slumped on the floor. 'Cor, I'm hungry, when's breakfast?' she asked, popping half a Twix in her mouth as she passed the black comb to Susan.

'Oh tuh! There's no mirror in here,' sighed Susan.

'Why are you so bothered about your hair all of a sudden? It doesn't look much different to how it always looks,' said Pauline, wearily.

'Hmm, I'll allow that very cheeky comment, due to the fact that you've just been rudely woken up!' said Susan crossly, as she began to tackle the overnight tangles.

'I've been trying to think about what we are doing here?' said Susan, tossing her head upside down in an attempt to detangle the long hair in the nape of her neck. 'Blimey,' she screeched, as a big lug of hair came out with the comb. 'I must brush it more often. Sorry Peewee, I've broken three prongs with that last tackle.'

'Oh Susan,' cried Pauline, now fully awake. 'Bring your own in future!' she said furiously, snatching it out of Susan's hand.

'Oooh, soreee!' retorted Susan, now very head sore, but looking more like a human being. Pauline carefully inspected the comb as Susan continued in her thoughts. 'I mean, I know we're here on a mission, but it doesn't really seem an important one, 'cos I can't remember what it is,' she said, looking out of the window.

'No, I know what you mean,' yawned Pauline. 'I can remember Mixy Lune, we've met him, and something about a key.'

'Oh yeah,' replied Susan, matter of factly. 'It's missing isn't it and someone thinks it could be here.'

'Hasn't Erasmus Drab pinched it?' corrected Pauline.

'Well, that's what we've been told, but He seems so nice to everyone, remember, giving out free food to all the village folk?'

'Which reminds me,' said Pauline, adjusting her cardigan. 'Where's our breakfast served?'

'C'mon,' said Susan, motivated by hunger. 'Let's find Captain Bossy Boots. He'll know where everything is, as usual.' They passed two more large pictures of Erasmus Drab in the corridor as they headed towards Dean's room. Knocking loudly got them nowhere, so they tried the door.

'Locked,' huffed Pauline.

'Typical cub scout antics,' said Susan. 'Protect your surroundings in an unknown land.'

'Oh well, let's go down for some food anyway,' said Pauline, her tummy rumbling rather loudly. At the bottom of the stairs, a small man in a white frilly hat pointed them in the right direction. Upon entering the large, empty room, full of black and white panelled walls, something good hit their nostrils.

'You could play chess all over these walls,' said Pauline, 'the floor even, wow, it's so shiny too.'

'I find chess so boring,' said Susan, taking a seat where the same small man showed her.

'You can't play, that's why,' said Pauline, sitting opposite.

'I don't want to play because it's BORING!' retorted Susan, defensively.

'NO, it's not boring,' Pauline carried on. 'You just have to have the ability to think ahead three or four moves, and that takes intelligence.'

'Hey, I passed my eleven plus, so don't say I'm thick,' Susan shouted back. The food arrived at that moment, which ended the argument nicely. Porridge sat in the black shiny bowls. It had smelt much better than it looked, but then lots of things smell good when you're starving. Hot lemon was on offer from a silver-grey lopsided teapot.

'No bacon and eggs then,' scowled Susan. They ate the lot though, then continued to argue for several minutes about each other's annoying habits.

'What time is it?' asked Pauline of the small man in the white cap and frilly edged apron.

'One hundred and three moments since the third sun rise,' came his precise reply.

'What the heck does that tell me?' cried Pauline, rudely. 'I need to know in hours and minutes,' she said, shaking her hands.

'Where's Dean, anyway? I knew he'd mess up somehow,' moaned Susan impatiently, picking up her juice. 'He thinks he knows everything that lad, and where is he now when we need him?'

'Goodness knows!' sighed Pauline, equally frustrated.

'What do we need him for anyway?' Susan suddenly announced. 'We can carry on without him.'

'Yeah,' agreed Pauline, finishing her drink.

'More juice, Peewee?' Susan asked, relaxing back into her chair.

'This juice is rather good. When we've finished shall we have another look around the shops?' Pauline replied.

'What a good idea, I wonder what they use for money? I fancy a few things I saw.'

'It's all free,' Pauline reminded her, sharply.

Susan and Pauline took their time at the dining table, unaware that they had both become totally distracted from the task in hand. Time was ticking on. For the girls - they couldn't work out how much. For Dean – he was totally unaware of his dangerous situation. He was in a deep sleep, locked in his room upstairs, unable to be reached by Mixy, who had by now, slipped back into his humdrum habits of dreariness.

Drab's scheme had worked beautifully. They would soon all be contracted into the daily routine of Drabacus. Totally relying on Him for survival, unable and unwilling to think for themselves. Content to be controlled, due to lack of appetite for life. It worked every time visitors arrived. It never needed much to change harmony into discord, diverting people's attention wherever He wanted. They became like putty in His hands, to make of them what He pleased. In a few more hours, His guests would have forgotten why they ever came, and the doors to the Erasmotel could be unlocked to allow themselves into thinking that they were in control.

The next part of His plan could now be put into action and Erasmus Drab began to get very excited as He approached the lake. His elegant transport came to a stop and he stepped out to survey the familiar island. Without any effort, he popped off the carriage roof to reveal an 'uber cool' boat as it was placed upside down on the water's edge. He rowed over with ease, his face full of mischief.

19

MUSIC TO THEIR EARS

The moments passed on. However, Dean had begun to stir. In the distant hills, something was happening. The blaze of colour and vibrant chord of music came riding over the wind like a wave washing out a mud-filled corner of a gully. A parade of animals followed a lone traveller dancing about, creating the atmosphere of a carnival. The tiny, but noisy procession got nearer. People nearby were captivated by its brightness, and began to stare in awe at the positively cheery sight. As the foreigner reached Drab's Erasmotel, the music floated up, passing the window of the unknown prison that Dean slept in. A familiar tune entered Dean's head, bringing him out of his slumber.

SCOOBY DOOBY DOO, WHERE ARE YOU, YOU'VE GOT SOME WORK TO DO NOW.

The melody lingered around his brain, immediately switching him on. He sat up, singing along on autopilot, and found himself jumping out of bed and racing to the window. He laughed out loud as he recognised the small, jolly character leading the fanfare. It was Michael, his brother, along with Frilly, the two rabbits Bosun and Leo, Meedo, Jobim and the rest of the monkeys. The colour radiating from them hit the back of Dean's eyes like a fluorescent hammer. Michael was so bright and cheery. His presence was striking, and the music his favourite, 'Scooby Doo' the cartoon character, guaranteed to bring anyone out of the deepest coma. Dean tried his door. It was locked. He returned to the window, finding it unlocked, and using sheets from his bed, shimmied down to greet his little brother with a big hug.

'Dean, you're so pale,' yelled Michael. 'What happened? All the colour has drained out of you. You look like a victim of Dracula!'

Wow,' said Dean, as he looked down and compared himself to Michael. 'I hadn't noticed, in fact I've only just woken up. Yikes!' he screamed, as he looked at his watch. 'It's seven o'clock, our time. We've got to be back for nine!' As the 'Blue Peter' theme tune shrilled out from the tiny cassette recorder, Michael began to tell Dean of Mixy's worry when they entered the Erasmotel.

'Mixy became anxious when you all became tired and began to argue. He sent Frilly back to the lake. Meedo and Jobim found the boat and told Maddison how Drab's power was overcoming you. Maddison came to my room in the middle of the night and woke me up, giving me the shock of my life, especially when he spoke. I wasn't frightened though because I thought I was in a dream! He explained where you'd gone and said we needed something to refresh your spirits and remind you of home, to give you the power to regain your own will. At first, Maddison just wanted me to come and get you and bring you back. Then he suggested that I bring our big Christmas present from Mum and Dad, with all our favourite songs and tunes we've recorded from the telly. These should keep us on track until we get back and we've completed the mission. What do you think?'

'Michael, you're brilliant! We've got to get the girls. If you're right, they'll be like me, totally unaware of their situation.' Young Michael was in his element. Like a proud peacock showing off his feathers – impressing his big brother was a rare thing and he made the most of it, reminding Dean constantly for the next few minutes, wasn't it good that he'd thought to bring the tape recorder on holiday?

Going around to the front door, they passed the dining room window where Susan and Pauline were still chatting at the table. Michael blasted out the title song to 'Banana Splits'.

TRA LA LA, LA LA LA LAA, TRA LA LA, LALALALAAAA.

Dean and Michael sang in accompaniment. 'Four bananas, three bananas, two bananas, one, all bananas sitting in the bright summer sun.'

The girls looked towards the window, then they suddenly dashed over. Michael's radiance was stunning against the backdrop of grey gloom. The colour radiating from him passed through the glass, making it shatter instantly. The colour wrapped around them like a blanket, soaking into their pale skin. Then the dancing started, as if a spell had been broken, because all four began jumping around like mad clowns, singing along to the well-known tunes. 'Stop the Pigeon' was next, with Dean adding a superb Mutley laugh at the end. Within minutes everyone was being restored. Michael continued to explain Drab's strategy, which Maddison had told him in great detail, now obvious by the grade of colour they had all become.

'He lulls you into a false sense of security, then with the power of suggestion, He stops you thinking for yourself, only believing what you're told. The inner laziness in people comes out and it's at this point where everything seems too much trouble.'

'Yes, do you remember Drab told us we were fitting in nicely?' said Pauline, remembering that His words had niggled her at the time.

'Yeah, then everything in the market was free, making you think that He is really kind…I even began to doubt that He could have stolen the key, He seemed so wonderful,' commented Susan.

'Then we all started arguing,' nodded Dean. 'Only seeing the bad faults in each other.'

Michael interrupted. 'That's when you stopped working as a team and He was able to separate Dean, who is in charge of the time.'

'Hmm, and without his leadership and organisation, Pauline and I just sat about content to do nothing, not realising that in a few hours we would be well and truly trapped here,' added Susan, with a chill.

'We've got to think positive,' said Dean, now fully revitalised. 'The colour is coming back in you two – get listening and remembering a few more good tunes, and get some more chocolate. When you're full of 'Technicolour' we'll get going. We've just under two hours to get to the castle and see if the key is there,' said Dean, setting his watch to buzz an hour before they needed to return. Susan and Pauline just had time to finish off their well-rehearsed routine of a Scottish jig to the tune of 'Blue Peter' before Dean decided they were OK.

'Frilly, where is Mixy at the moment?' asked Dean of the little deer.

'He's gone back home after collecting his food. He will have forgotten all about you three by now, that's why he asked me to go and get help before you went to sleep, because he recognised what was happening to himself.'

They set off back to Mixy's house, and without knocking, they entered, giving Mixy a shock which soon disappeared as he also got an injection of joy. Being inspired, he once more began to help the children on their quest. After an introduction to Michael, and several pieces of chocolate, they all set off towards the castle.

Meanwhile, Maddison sat patiently waiting at the doors of the lift, pondering the rescue plan he had sent Michael to execute. It was all he could hope for. Suddenly, he realised he was not alone, as the handsome form of Erasmus Drab came forward out of the shadows. Drat, thought Drab, as he clocked the monkey standing in his way. Maddison stood to his feet, his move taking the unwelcome visitor by surprise, just a little.

'Are you lost little monkey?' he asked sweetly, stepping forward as if to offer help. 'Let me guide you to the lake,' he said in a fatherly voice, offering out his manicured hand. Maddison stretched out both arms and legs to the side in the shape of a cross, completely blocking the entrance with his body. This resistance from Maddison was unexpected by Drab. He was used to getting his own way here in Drabacus.

'You're surely not going to stop me coming in, are you?' he protested. 'I mean, you can't hold your arms and legs in that position forever, can you monkey?'

'What do you want Erasmus Drab – to steal and spoil some more?' Maddison voiced, powerfully. His ability to speak was a revelation to his foe. Drab knew in an instant he had met his match and stepped back to reassess his position.

'So, you know who I am and my past crime – interesting – I won't deny it. I would have returned it had you let me back,' he droned, pacing the narrow cave from side to side. 'I'm presuming it is you who has been thwarting my attempts all these years?'

'Why *did* you take that key?' asked Maddison boldly, remaining steadfast in the doorway.

'I really don't know,' he grimaced. 'It's in my nature I suppose – I can't help it – nobody's perfect, are they?' pronounced Drab, suggesting Maddison had faults too.

'No,' confessed Maddison, quickly. 'But the difference is we don't often recognise when we are doing wrong, but *you* – you are wilful – you *know* beforehand the damage you do and you don't care who gets hurt along the way,' he replied intensely.

'You are missing the point, dear monkey,' he waxed lyrically. 'It's *interesting* seeing people deal with disappointment. I'm building their character as they adjust to misfortune. Let folks have things *too* easy and they don't appreciate things. Greater satisfaction is always achieved when obstacles have been overcome. Trust me, I've been around for a long time now. I'm doing them a favour really,' he finished indignantly, placing his hands on his hips.

Maddison processed the half-truth on offer for a moment, then replied. 'That's your opinion only – I don't share your training methods Erasmus Drab, they bring unnecessary pain and suffering.' Drab sighed out loud, releasing his hands to express his frustration.

'Why, oh why, am I always so misunderstood? It was only a key, monkey – by the way – what's your name?'

'I'm not giving you the privilege of using it, Drab.'

'Why not? You know mine. I'm sure if you got to know me better, you'd soon see I'm not as bad as you're making me out,' smiled Erasmus Drab.

'Just a key from up there, maybe,' said Maddison, pointing upwards in the lift. 'But here in Abacus, you have totally destroyed the once happy community that existed here. I don't know exactly how, but I just know in my heart it's YOU!'

'What an accusation to make with no proof, very judgmental of you monkey, if you don't mind me saying.'

Maddison's arms began to ache as he heard Drab's allegation, and he lowered them slightly to rest them on the metal guards, a move not unnoticed by Drab.

'I see you're getting tired now monkey, c'mon let me through. I don't want to knock you out of the way – but I will if I have to,' he said, ending sternly.

As quick as a flash, Maddison drew the metal guards shut, pressing the lift button in firmly at the same time. As it began to move upwards, Drab's hands attempted to prise them open, but Maddison roared as he went in to bite them, forcing him off, as he continued to hold in the button in order for the lift to rise. He stopped the lift just before the ground floor, leaving a gap of six inches in which to spy down on Drab, who looked up at the triumphant Maddison peering through the narrow slot. Drab kept his cool and walked underneath the mysterious gateway, carefully examining the floor of the metal box, now completely out of reach. He walked back out of the empty space.

'Stalemate for now then, monkey – but you will *have* to lower it again for the children's return and I am patient, very very patient. So I'll just wait here with you.' Maddison became worried for the first time. Drab had the upper hand and he knew it!

20

A PAST CHALLENGE COMES IN HANDY!

Soon, the turrets of the castle could be clearly seen beyond dull, withered trees. Michael gave everyone a short burst of tunes along the way, causing great laughter from Mixy, as Susan, Pauline and Michael couldn't help dancing along. Dean explained to Michael that they had found part of an ancient rhyme, called The Sanguine, which had energised Mixy for a short time upon reading it.

'We need to find it, if at all possible,' said Dean. 'It could be the key to giving these people back their will to live life to the full, and recognise Drab for what He is – a thief, NOT a giver, which is what He kids everyone into thinking.'

Then Pauline had a thought. 'You know the bit of rhyme we found on the stone which was on the map – is there another stone in Abacus which may contain more of it that Drab may have missed?'

'Yes, there are two ancient stones,' replied Mixy. 'But the other is located at the other side of the castle. You wouldn't have time to get in, get the key and check that out too, before you have to get back home.'

'No, but YOU would have time to go and have a look,' suggested Dean, taking out the piece of paper with the tiny portion of The Sanguine copied onto it. He handed it to Mixy. 'Now you've got a little bit to keep yourself. You could look with Frilly – she'll come back and report if you get held up by Drab's influence.'

'Splendid,' he said, taking the rhyme from Dean.

Mixy and the animals went around the castle, after pointing to a possible way in. Although it was not guarded at all, there was no way across the large moat which surrounded it. The water swirled at high speed.

'I wonder how deep this water is?' said Susan, anxiously peering over the edge. Dean, having found a stick, was already dipping it in trying to measure its depth.

'About three foot, I reckon,' he replied, thoughtfully. 'If we all hold on to each other, we should be able to work through the force of the water and cross easily.'

'Oh, I hate getting wet,' cried Susan. 'It had better be warm.'

'Just think, S, you'll not need a bath 'till October,' joked Pauline, knowing Susan's hatred of water.

With solid determination, the quartet stepped into the whirling moat, hands clasped tightly, with Dean leading the way. The water gushed up to their waists, its temperature on the chilly side, causing a few 'oohs' and 'aaghs' as it hit them initially. The noise of the water became the feature of the crossing, drowning out any speech. The water got lower and lower as they crossed. It was only knee high by the time they reached the other side. It was all over in thirty five seconds, with both girls keeping their long hair dry. They began to feel cold as soon as they climbed the bank at the other side.

'Bbrr,' chattered Susan's teeth.

'C'mon, keep moving, it's the only way to keep warm, said Dean, robustly.

The grey, grassy bank quickly led to a wide gravel path laid towards the entrance of the castle. Its whole appearance was shiny as you got up close. The building materials used were unfamiliar. Only one of its three turrets was visible, to the left, high above them. The archway before them was six feet in thickness, making a nice porch, which sheltered them from the light wind, which on wet clothes made for a chill. The tall walls, coloured grey with black lines here and there, giving a marble effect, had a glossy texture. Michael couldn't help but dig his nail in, to make a mark in it. It so reminded him of a candle waiting to be scraped into little flakes. His little face lit up with glee when it did so, as his index fingernail dragged down. Blocking the archway, was a matching sturdy door, ten feet in height. It didn't go all the way up to the top of the arch, but left a gap of about two feet. With the walls of the castle extending as far as the eye could see, there was no option but to gain entry this way. In one piece, the door stretched across the archway with no handle clear to view. It wasn't ever meant to open. No-one was ever meant to enter. Nothing about on the ground was going to help them gain entry.

'If one of us could get over, maybe we could figure a way in and out,' said Dean.

'I know,' announced Susan, loudly, 'we could make a tower of people, like they do in the circus. The last person to reach the top being you. Hopefully, you'll be able to scramble over.'

'Yeah, but how will Dean get to the top of us?' Pauline asked, thoughtfully.

'If you be the anchor person, Pauline, standing face to the door,' gestured Dean, catching Susan's idea in his head. 'Susan, you will climb and stand on her shoulders. Michael and I will hoist you up. You will also lean with your face to the door, then Michael, you make a lean-to on Pauline's shoulders. I'll climb on your back and onto your shoulders to get a good lift up to Susan.'

'Blimey, I'm glad you know what you're doing, 'cos I didn't follow a word of that,' laughed Susan, optimistically.

'You'll see it coming together,' said Dean, confidently.

'No we won't, 'cos we'll have our noses squashed into that door,' smiled Pauline, ever hopeful of Dean's plan.

'We have done this kind of thing before, remember the lift door…' Dean tailed off quickly, remembering that Michael knew nothing about that little adventure.

'Don't remind me, my back still has your foot imprinted on it!' said Susan, in a whisper.

'Anyway, back to the plan. While I'm climbing up, it'll get a bit jittery, but I'll be fast. And Micky, you'll need to keep the girls steady.'

'Let's go for it,' Michael nodded, pleased at being an important part of the plan. The practice proved to be difficult, Susan being unable to steady her upper body as Dean clambered on her back. Down they tumbled on to Pauline and Michael. 'You know,' said Michael, inspecting the wall again, 'it's a bit like wax, this wall. Couldn't we carve some out to make footholds and handles?'

'Great idea,' they replied. Dean's knife was out in a flash, sinking easily into the clay-like structure. Within ten minutes, four handholds and two footholds had made it easy for the girls to steady themselves against the door. Uttering mild apologies for clutching hold of Susan too tightly, Dean managed to get his arms over the door and was able to hoist himself over, after lunging from Susan's sore shoulders, causing her to yell loudly.

What was over the other side surprised him with great relief. Instead of a large drop down, the ground was only two feet away. Kidding the others it would be a death-defying leap, but he would attempt it as any hero would, he acted out the perfect gymnastic landing. The door was actually giving the illusion that it was impossible to enter to the outsider.

From the inside, it was obvious that the door couldn't open, so there had to be another way out. It wasn't long before Dean, ignoring cries of 'what can you see?' and 'are you alright?' from the others, noticed two tunnels in the side of the wall. One contained steps, the other looking like the inside of a giant swimming pool fun slide. He tiptoed down the grey, waxy steps making no noise, coming out around the corner, behind the others, who still had their heads stretched up to see if Dean would appear. They were a little disturbed, not having heard him for about a minute now. With a quick whistle, he caught their attention.

21

AWESOME WONDER

No-one had thought of looking for another means of entry. Well, why would they suspect an easy way in? The tunnels were covered by illandrium bushes, which had not lost their sweet smell. Like they'd just found a pound, the others followed Dean back up the steps. A marbled courtyard met them at the top, laid with alternating grey and black tiles. No-one was about and the air felt eerie, as the wind began to blow its full course. The light rain it had brought landed on the children as they looked for a door.

The last two tasks had tired everyone. So Michael decided to play the theme tune from 'Stop the Pigeon', which cheered everyone up, taking away the fear that was building, in an instant. They headed towards a large, white arched door, overlooked by two gargoyles that looked down upon them menacingly. It was slightly ajar and so in they went, treading lightly.

'Where to now?' asked Pauline, as she stared around the vast hallway. Knotted wood panelled the walls, stretching twenty feet up to the ceiling. On each panel hung a large portrait of Erasmus Drab in a different pose. To the east, stretching from the floor to the ceiling, was a large stained glass window, framed with thick, velvet curtains. Large, metal birds of prey sat on a pedestal in each corner of this square room. Five doors presented themselves.

'Let's each of us check a door and report back by the time you've sung the theme tune to 'Banana Splits' in your head,' suggested Dean. They all chose a door, leaving the fifth for a joint look. Three of the doors led to other finely decorated grey rooms. Behind Michael's lay stone steps, leading upwards in a circle of darkness. This must be one of the turrets, he thought, running the shape of the castle through his head. Obeying Dean's instruction, he returned to the others, not before running up several steps to see how far he could see. Dean had already gestured to the girls to explore the fifth door after his findings. Michael was pleased to report something different behind his. Behind the fifth door lay a grand dining table, made of glass. It was laid with fine china and glassware, set for a party of four. In black bowls sat fresh, steaming hot soup. The aroma drifted quickly up eight nostrils.

'This looks like another ploy to hold us up, I'm sure,' said Pauline, as Michael marched towards the table, his tummy rumbling. Susan quickly got out a couple of Twix bars, which quickly diverted their attention back to finding the key.

'All our rooms were empty, yeah?' questioned Dean, as he bit into his. 'I mean, there's no drawers or cupboards to hide a key in?'

'No, the rooms were empty, apart from the walls having Drab's face plastered all over them,' confirmed Pauline. Susan nodded to indicate the same, her mouth full of chocolate. All four headed towards the steps Michael had found. No windows lit the circular staircase. They began to climb in the dark, around and around the turret of steps.

'Does this remind you of anything?' said Susan, as she clumped around in the dark. The stone steps were about one foot apart, which actually made it a little easier, as did

Michael's matches, lighting the way on and off. Eventually it began to get lighter, as they could see an end to the steps. A sense of unease filled them as they reached the top. They were not alone. Two white, Alsatian dogs were sat waiting outside a black, arched door. Real ones! They began to growl as the children left the last step.

'Good doggie,' was Dean's friendly greeting. 'Play some music Michael, it might distract them.' Pauline instinctively took a risk and with one hand outstretched, tried coaxing a lick out of the first one. In an instant, both became like puppies, rolling over for a belly tickle.

'Everything seems dangerous or misleading, but it isn't when you challenge it. It's an interesting pattern,' concluded Susan. 'Now, what's behind this door?'

The view from the window at the top of the tower held their attention for only a second, as they pondered whether Erasmus Drab might be behind the door. 'Supposing He is in here, are we ready to face Him?' asked Dean, cautiously.

'I wanna see Him,' said Michael, excitedly.

'You've seen Him, His flippin' picture is all over the place,' said Pauline.

'I'm not frightened of Him,' he went on. 'Susan said He's ok really.'

'Yeah, that's when I wasn't myself. He's very cunning, Michael. It's all been a bit too easy so far, don't you think?' said Susan, raising her bushy eyebrows at Pauline and Dean.

'Michael, set the recorder on all our favourite tunes on side 'A', they're the most vibrant,' instructed Dean. 'If Drab is in here, just press the play button fast!' All of them held their breath as Dean took hold of the ornate handle and pressed down to release the catch. The dogs started barking as if to give warning to someone. Dean cautiously slid his head around the door, only to be met with wonder! 'Wow!' he cried loudly, opening the door wider.

'What, what?' cried Susan and Pauline, frantically. Michael dived in below Dean's waist.

'Smart,' he drooled, his eyes scanning the well-lit room.

They slowly entered the large, circular hideaway. The white walls had a golden glow – something not grey at last! They were reflecting the radiating beauty from all manner of objects in the room. Each item sat on a white, marble pedestal, three-feet in height. The colours were amazing. Shiny red rubies, blue sapphires and green emeralds studded a golden crown on one. A live, tropical bird with feathers of rich reds, blues and yellows sat patiently, blinking every five seconds, in a large, ornate, golden cage on another. On the next lay an enormous book, its pages making a wedge six inches thick, with a brown, leather cover inlaid with gold lettering bearing the words 'THE TRUTH'. The next pedestal held a clear, diamond-shaped glass box, holding an intricately carved crystal, glistening and twinkling with the most fantastic range of colours ever seen, as light bounced off it from the four, large, arched windows. Several other pedestals held other items of interest and beauty. Cries of delight and wonder filled the air. The girls were drawn to the jewellery, the boys to the magnificent bird.

'Just look at all this, what is it and why is it all in colour?' said Pauline, puzzled.

'Why is it all here?' questioned Dean.

'There's loads of things,' replied Susan. 'Look at this golden statue of a maiden, playing a harp thing. It reminds me of the Oscars in Hollywood. Hey, there's even some markings underneath, but they're not English.'

'Look at this,' said Michael excitedly, taking hold of a slim, silver, metallic box. 'I think it opens up – oh wow! It's like a typewriter but with a TV screen in its lid – I wonder what it could be?'

'Let's have a look,' said Dean, ever the electronics wizard. 'Does it have a button?'

'No, just this button on its own in the corner. Should I push it?'

'Give it here,' said Dean, enthusiastically. Quickly examining all the buttons, he plumped for the one in the corner and suddenly there was a noise, which made them jump. The screen lit up and displayed fish swimming about in a mock tank. A small, multi-coloured apple sat in the top left hand corner. Susan and Pauline now joined the boys.

'What is it?' Susan asked, excitedly. As Dean tapped his fingers over the keys, nothing happened. He suggested that it looked like a futuristic computer, like from Star Trek, the popular science fiction programme. 'Where is it from, do you wonder?' said Susan, a big fan of the show. 'The Klingon Empire,' she suggested, in a made up voice.

'Dunno,' replied Dean, captivated. 'It just says 'MacBook Pro' here at the bottom of the screen. Dean began to get frustrated at not being able to unlock its secrets, and passed it back to Michael to fathom out, his eyes now drawn to items on the wall. Inside a glass case, on one wall, hung two frames. One contained a picture of a beautiful lady on a summer's day, in a gorgeous ruffled dress with a parasol, standing in green grass. Someone called Monet had signed it in the corner at the bottom. The other case held a piece of paper, which was edged in gold. The markings looked familiar.

'Look,' said Susan, excitedly. 'This could be 'The Sanguine'! Get out the paper we wrote the other bit on.'

'I gave it to Mixy,' Dean reminded her.

'Peewee, come and take a look, what d'ya think?' asked Susan, smiling.

Pauline was busy fishing around in a red velvet-lined bin, containing bits of metal. Pauline suddenly screamed with joy. 'I think I've found the key,' pulling out familiar bits she'd remembered from the line drawings in the library. 'See, this is the head piece!' Dean dashed over and together they lifted down the container.

'Looks like Drab couldn't piece it all together,' he laughed.

'Three, four, five, six, and two pieces back home, eight all together – they're all here, yippee,' shouted Pauline, elated at achieving the goal.

'Look at this, P,' said Susan again, 'is this it d'ya think?' as she took down the heavy frame from its case.

'Yes, definitely,' she confirmed. 'I recognise that series of squiggles there and there. Mixy IS going to be pleased.'

Dean announced, 'this room is like an Aladdin's cave. We know these two things are precious,' he said of The Sanguine markings and the key. Maybe everything in this room is, we just don't know from where.'

'I know,' Susan sighed, walking over to the lonely bird. 'I wish we could return him, he looks so unhappy.'

'You can,' he squawked unexpectedly, making Susan jump and squeal at the same time. 'You have all been so excited, you didn't hear me shouting for the last few moments,' he said frustrated, but mellowing immediately in his next sentence. All four gathered around the cage. He opened his bright, pink beak and twinkled his bright, green eyes. 'You have not much time. Erasmus Drab will be here in a few moments to feed and tempt me.'

Michael frowned, asking 'tempt you to what?'

'To tell Him how to open many doors to different worlds, including mine. But I will not,' squawked the beautiful bird, ruffling his feathers slightly.

'What does He say to tempt you?' questioned Pauline.

'He says He will let me out of this cage and I will be able to fly around. But who wants to look at this grey and dreary landscape all day anyway? Plus, He will not keep his word – He never does – do not believe a single word He says. He is a well-known liar,' said the tropical bird, with firm belief.

'We can let you out, can't we?' said Susan, looking up and down for a door.

'Probably, but I have been here for so long, my wings will not be strong enough to fly right away,' he replied.

'Have you got a name?' asked Dean, going on quickly to introduce him and the others.

'I am Kyzer, 'Emperor of the Air''. My world is full of my kind and the doorway is in the centre of Abacus, as are many more, but Erasmus Drab must never find this out. I flew here by mistake and decided to explore for a while. Erasmus Drab tricked me into this cage and I have been here for such a long time now.'

'Why are you in colour and everything else is drained of it?' asked Michael.

'I'm not sure, but I think it's because I have the ability to remember things very easily, and I just keep reminding myself of all the good things I know, and keep hoping that one day I will be rescued,' he offered as an explanation.

'That fits in with our theory,' said Dean, explaining the use of the tape recorder and Michael's rescue earlier.

'This key is from our world, called Earth,' Pauline informed him. 'We've come to get it back.'

'Yes, and this…' added Susan, taking the rhyme out of its frame, '…is a special, ancient script which Drab has banned in Abacus, making everything Drabacus. The people here have forgotten to have fun, communicate, trust or have hope.

If folk here get this back, maybe they can return to full colour and get a life!' exclaimed Susan excitedly to Kyzer.

Just then Dean's watch beeped. 'Right, that's just one hour before the door closes!' Everyone got into first gear, realising that time was now the enemy.

'For some reason, I can't open this blinkin' cage,' said Dean, fiddling with the door. 'But we'll defo take you with us if you want, Kyzer. We can't take everything, so we'll take everything we know doesn't belong to Drab. That's our key, the script and Kyzer, agreed?' said Dean, organising the trip back. All nodded, especially Kyzer, who let out a long, loud squawk of delight.

The birdcage was awkward to carry and so the two boys shared the task. Susan and Pauline led the way, with the bucket of key pieces and script rolled up in Susan's pocket. Michael decided to play some music to gee everyone up, but there was no need. Their hearts were racing with excitement at what they had found and were now taking away from the castle without permission. They were also aware that they could run into Erasmus Drab at any moment.

22

STEPPING UP

Dean checked his watch again. 'We've just under one hour to get back,' he announced. 'We'd better hurry.'

The dogs that had been patiently sitting outside the door, ran ahead down the steps. The children had more difficulty, having to time the steps in the dark. Pauline took charge of match-lighting duties. They only had five matches, each lasting only fifteen seconds at best. As Pauline went to strike the last match, there was an almighty screech and crash from behind. Realising someone was falling into her and Susan, she steadied herself, and flung out her hands into the dark in an attempt to catch whoever it was.

Dean had missed his footing, not adjusting to the curved angle of the step. He went tumbling past her, knocking Susan roughly to the side. Dean had continued to cling onto the bulky cage, but somehow Pauline managed to grab it. The harsh sounds of Dean crashing down the steps told them he would be injured to some degree. He had practically rolled right down to the bottom of the steps, at least twenty, collapsing into a splodge at the bottom. Michael began to cry. Here they were, for a few frightening moments, in the pitch black, not knowing the outcome of Dean's rough tumble. The matches were spent. The darkness made it impossible to rush to his aid. The only thing they could do was tread very carefully, slowly feeling their way down the remaining staircase, shouting words of comfort to Dean to indicate they would soon be with him.

Pauline took over carrying the cage with Michael at the back. It was a tense time, the climb down seemed to take for ever and no reply from Dean could be heard. Susan was the first to see him lying still on the floor, his limbs twisted this way and that. His head was bleeding and his face was scraped from where he'd bounced off the walls.

'Dean, Dean,' she gently shook him to get a response. She knew enough about first aid to know not to move him, and began to regret not taking the free first aid course last spring, with her friend, Kay. She began to panic. 'Peewee, he's breathing but unconscious,' she shouted back up the steps. Pauline eventually joined her to inspect the injuries. Michael rushed over to his brother.

'Dean would know what to do,' sobbed Michael, frustrated and upset at the sight of his big brother's limp body. Hidden skills would now come into practice as the girls, both ex-Brownie Guides, began to check for broken limbs. Susan checked his spine and neck. Both seemed to be intact.

'Right,' sighed Susan, taking charge as she reached into her back pocket. 'Michael take The Sanguine and go and find Mixy. Tell him what's happened and let's hope he can help.'

There was one good thing to come out of the fall, however. The cage had become disjointed at the door, as it jolted into the wall before Pauline had caught it. It was now busted open and Kyzer walked out, squawking with delight. 'Take Kyzer with you,' said Pauline, thoughtfully. 'He can rest on your arm and flex his wings for later on.'

'I am sorry, I cannot help here,' squealed Kyzer, saddened his new friend was hurt. 'But I know the area and I will help Michael find his way around quickly.'

'Leave the recorder, Michael,' requested Pauline. 'Do you think you can keep all the songs in your head?'

'Let's play them again,' suggested Susan, taking hold of Dean's hand. 'Kyzer, try and learn these songs to sing to Michael.' And so they did, with mixed feelings, as Dean lay lifeless at the bottom of the steps in the grand hall.

'Blast,' shouted Pauline, frantically. 'Dean's watch has got smashed in the fall, we don't know what time we have left.'

'He said we'd just got under one hour, about ten minutes ago,' said Susan. 'I'll just have to rely on my inner clock,' she said, confidently. 'Michael, if you can't find Mixy right away, you MUST return to the cave and get back home. That way, if anything goes wrong here, you'll be able to tell my Mum and Dad where we are…'

'Susan!' cried Pauline, drawing on her inner reserve. 'Don't be so pessimistic, we're gonna get back, RIGHT!'

'P, I'm just planning ahead as usual, don't panic.'

Giving Michael a reassuring hug, they sent him on his vital mission. Upset, but determined, he set off towards the moat with gusto, singing the 'Wacky Races' theme tune, with trills from Kyzer, catching hold of the tunes already.

Back in the cave, the stand-off continued. Erasmus Drab had talked continuously, trying his best to convince the monkey that he had him wrong. Truth be told, Maddison was beginning to feel the effects of Drab's lies. The onslaught of words had lasted almost two of earth's hours, which in Drabacus seemed a lifetime! His mental strength was draining fast as he tried to resist entering into a debate with

Drab that may entice him to lower the lift. He had tried to keep remembering the facts he *knew*, refreshing them in his head, to bat away the train of thought trying to pierce his intellect.

As Drab droned on and on, suddenly there was a faint noise at the cave entrance. Drab quickly hid down a separate corridor as Jobim and Meedo ran furiously into the cave, both shouting. 'Maddison, Maddison, something wonderful is happening here in Drabacus. People are starting to sing! Singing – it's wonderful,' Meedo blurted, out of breath.

'And dancing again,' added Jobim.

Erasmus Drab's face twisted in the shadows at the unwanted news. He was out of there like a bolt of lightning!

Noticing Drab had left, Maddison lowered the lift to greet his family members. His brain hurt with the monologue Drab had performed. The intervention by Meedo and Jobim was the miracle he needed to hear and replenish his spirit. Could he now dare to believe that he would be able to return and live in a restored Abacus with his beloved family? His excitement rose as he continued to wait for the children's return.

Back at the castle, vital minutes were draining away as the girls remained with Dean. 'Come on Dean, please wake up,' pleaded Susan, knowing how much she had come to rely on him over the last few hours. His authority and command was a security blanket, sadly now not available to either of the girls.

'Let's put him in the recovery position,' suggested Pauline, remembering the first aid procedure. The manoeuvre involved turning Dean onto his left side. As they did, he began to stir slightly.

'Dean, Dean, are you ok?' whispered Susan anxiously in his ear. Pauline touched his shoulder gently and repeated the question. 'It's a good sign he came round a bit then…at least I think so, from what I remember,' Susan added.

'He may just be a bit dazed,' Pauline said, looking around. 'If we can get him awake, we can start to get out of here…Uh Oooh Chungo!' she suddenly said, changing the pattern of her voice.

Susan instinctively looked up – she knew trouble had arrived.

23

OF COURSE IT COULDN'T BE THAT EASY!

Behind them stood Erasmus Drab. He had appeared from nowhere. Towering above them, He had the appearance of a mysterious prince from a bygone era, with a cunning smile sweeping His face. His shadow touched Pauline's knee as she crouched by Dean. His flowing, black, silky coat dropped to the top of His long, black, silver-buckled boots. A white, ruffle-necked shirt, which had matching double cuffs, peeped out from the sleeves of His jacket, each holding a black, shiny cufflink, drawing attention to His long fingers and highly polished, black nails. He looked very different from the first encounter, the girls unfortunately now having time to study Him at close quarters. Seconds felt like minutes, as they became really afraid for the first time since entering Drabacus.

'Well, whom do I find here…in MY home?' came His powerful, questioning voice. He walked closer to the trio. Fear gripped both girls. They found they couldn't move, drawn in by His coal-black eyes, they were both rendered speechless. Drab first noticed the empty cage at the bottom of the steps, then the half-hidden bin, filled with key bits, another prized possession. For the first time, Susan noticed the gigantic mirror stretching right across the wall opposite, and could see a back view of Erasmus Drab's curly hair, dangling almost to His waist. Looking back to His face, His eyes suddenly pierced Susan, as He demanded to know where the bird was.

'He…he…didn't want to stay,' stammered Pauline, truthfully. Drab ignored her, and with His hands on His hips asked Susan what she was doing with *His* belongings.

Gaining a righteous inner confidence, she looked Him in the eyes and shakily replied, 'if you're talking about this key, it doesn't belong to you, and y'know it!' she ended sharply, and then began shaking slightly.

'Who says it doesn't?' He questioned.

Pauline mustered up the courage to reply. 'You were seen stealing these pieces from our world…'

'OUR world,' He interrupted, scornfully. 'YOUR world is MY world and mine is now yours,' He said, with open arms. 'Feel free to stay as long as you like.' And He laughed, wickedly. 'You are already beginning to feel at home again, I see,' as He swept his arms towards the large mirror, bringing a shock to the girls as they looked. Their reflections were pale and insipid, and the glimpse seemed to drain even more life out of them. 'Your plight is useless. You mortals are weak, and you will never get back to the doorway in time. Soon you'll forget you were ever there,' He sneered. 'Then you will be mine forever, another triumph,' He scowled.

'Play the tape, quickly,' cried Susan. Pauline seemed to fumble for ages before she pressed the 'play' button. The 'Banana Splits' theme tune rang out in the large, hollow hall. They began to sing, and Drab laughed. Much to their horror, He began singing along with them.

'Four bananas make a bunch and so do many more!' Drab ridiculed, loudly.

'How does He know our tune?' said Susan, astounded to hear Drab's dulcet tones.

'I don't know,' stammered Pauline, who started to feel the colour drain from her at His words. Susan looked at her friend in desperation.

'Peewee, you're not grey, I think He's just creating the illusion. Get singing – don't believe what He's saying. Remember what Maddison said,' Susan blurted out.

'Believe in ourselves and the truth will set us free,' recalled Pauline with a half-hopeful smile.

Turning to look back at the mirror, they saw the true picture of themselves, still bursting with colour. They danced around Dean, singing at top note. Drab got angry with this and disappeared in front of their eyes. The noise had disturbed Dean, slowly waking him. He came around in a daze to see the girls jigging away to 'Scooby Dooby Doo'. It was such a strange sight, he thought he was dreaming. Susan noticed Dean stir first, and dashed to attend to him. 'Dean, are you ok?' she asked. 'We've got to get back, we're running out of time,' she said, with urgency.

'My ankle hurts, and my arm, and my leg and my head.'

'Can you walk?' Pauline urged.

'Where's our kid?' inquired Dean, concerned not to see his brother.

'He's gone for help,' reassured Pauline. Suddenly, the music slowed down and tunes began twisting and groaning in a strange fashion.

'The batteries are going!' screamed Susan. 'What are we gonna do?' We need that to keep us sane!'

'We don't, Susan,' announced Pauline. 'You just think we do. We've got the ability to remember good things, let's do that now and bat things to each other as a reminder.' A quick tennis match of positive words ensued across the hall, as Dean began to recover, helped to his feet by Pauline.

The tape stopped playing altogether. From now on it was just their faith in each other that would have to carry them through.

Suddenly, Erasmus Drab reappeared again before them, parking a smile at Susan.

'Just ignore Him, Susan,' said Pauline. 'If we don't listen to Him, He can't hurt us.' As Pauline and Dean hobbled on ahead, He had already caught Susan's attention.

'Why do you think I want to hurt you?' He said, in a noticeably gentler voice. 'Let me attend to your friend, he seems to have hurt himself whilst stealing my bird.'

'We haven't stolen it, he didn't want to stay – and you're not keeping our key, either,' said Susan, indignantly.

'Aha, a little spirit – I like that, Susan. You are a very pretty girl. I'm very lonely here,' continuing His smile. 'You would make a good companion, I think,' nodded Drab, holding out His hand. 'Here, have some chocolate – it has a calming effect, I believe.' Their chocolate supply was now depleted, and Erasmus Drab's sudden change of behaviour, revealing His loneliness, flattered and confused Susan somewhat.

Pauline and Dean had now managed to shuffle nearly halfway across the hall. 'How can you help him?' she asked, taking the chocolate, unable to hear Pauline and Dean screaming at her to follow them.

'He's hurt very badly. He will always be lame if he returns and his head wound is serious. If he stays here, in a short while all pain ceases. Drabacus is a better place than planet Earth. No wars, nobody dying from food shortages. No arguments, everyone is content. No illness exists and you'll live forever.'

'Could I go home and see my family? she requested, as she opened the chocolate wrapper.

'Whenever you want, they could stay here at the castle.' Drab had tapped into Susan's hidden fears, desires and compassion for others.

'Ok then,' she snapped. Her decision was made rather too quickly, much to Pauline's and Dean's horror!

'What's happened to Susan?' asked Dean.

'I think He's hypnotised her. She's only seeing what He wants her to see and hear. I don't know how He's doing it, but we're in trouble if we can't get her attention. Susan, are you coming?' Pauline shouted, with Dean hanging around her neck.

'NO, I'm staying here with Erasmus and so should Dean. He will be better off here – you can see how ill he is, and he might die back home. Can't you see that?'

'He's lying, Susan,' said Dean. 'I'm feeling better every minute. Come with us – I suspect He can't keep you here against your will.' Drab put his hand on Susan's right shoulder.

'But it's better here,' she cried in earnest. 'No wars or famine.'

'No,' shouted Dean, 'but what He's not told you is, there is no inner peace either. No food shortages, but you can't call what He dishes out, food. It's not a pleasure to eat, just a means of survival.'

Pauline then butted in. 'No arguments because no-one talks to each other. Contentment because…because no-one knows any difference.'

Dean carried on, 'who wants to live like that forever? – it'd be a living Hell, don't you see?' he urged, now standing on his own two feet.

'But He said I can go home anytime and visit my Mum and Dad.'

'Susan, you'll not WANT to go home, you'll be trapped,' cried Dean, in desperation.

Pauline started to throw in all the good things she'd have back home, like friends sharing yummy sweets, walks in Hurstbrook woods with the sunshine warming her face. Seeing baby John grow up, and most of all, her own free will to choose.

'Maddison spoke the truth when he said, 'don't believe anything Drab tells you,' Susan, try to remember,' said Dean, battling for her freedom.

She has made her choice, you all have one,' said Drab now, walking in front of her to create a shield. He walked towards Dean, His next target. 'It would be so much easier here,' He said to Dean, holding out His hand and looking deep into his eyes. Erasmus Drab's power began to exhaust him in his weakened state. 'I'll teach you how to fly – just think of all the adventures you could have.' Already, every word Drab spoke had the hypnotic effect of convincing Dean to give in, and slowly take His hand. 'See how much better you feel now,' said Drab, sitting Dean down on a large wicker chair that had gone unnoticed. Drab now began to circle Pauline, and whilst catching her eye, asked how she proposed to leave when no exit door could be seen.

'Michael will be back with help at any minute,' she informed him, hopefully.

'Ooh, you mean the small boy I've already captured behind that door,' He scoffed loudly, as He pointed to another unnoticed feature of the hall. In the momentary quietness, Pauline was stricken with despair as she heard Michael's desperate pleas for freedom.

'Please, help me…Susan…Pauline…I'm locked in,' cried his small, forlorn voice.

Looking around in horror, all the other doors had disappeared from sight and a fog began to rise and fill the room from its four corners. Giving in to her fear of the unknown, Pauline was powerless to resist Drab's disagreeable option, and she returned to join the others. He turned to His first conquest.

'See how easy it is Susan, to control people. I am doing nothing but putting a small problem in their way or some longed-for desire in their grasp, and they are giving up their will, just like that!' He began to gesticulate with His elegant hands. 'It's self-inflicting. Your kind are so lazy at heart, always taking the easy role, so selfish – wanting to please yourself so much, it gets in the way of other's feelings and needs.' His mocking laugh echoed around the Great Hall, revealing His true, ugly nature at last.

'Now,' He said commandingly, to all three captives. 'You're mine for as long as I want you!' With His hands beckoning the willing prisoners, He turned towards the steps. 'Come, take your place in my Trophy Room. Your capture is sweet after all your efforts, and I want to gloat.' He began to lead them back up the dark, spiral staircase.

24

ALL IS REVEALED AT LAST (WELL, NOT QUITE EVERYTHING)

Powerless to resist, they began to climb the dark tower to the Trophy Room.

But suddenly outside, the air was filled with at first a hum, and then as it got nearer, a hundred voices could be heard, all singing with joy and laughter. Erasmus Drab ran over to a window overlooking the town. There, an army of villagers, slowly turning from grey to a multitude of colours, were fast marching upon the castle, carrying flags and waving banners in the air.

Without warning, the doors to the Great Hall burst wide open. There stood Michael, Mixy and Kyzer in full colour, singing The Sanguine on top note. Drab turned, horror across His face, as He heard the forbidden song ringing in His ears.

Seek to serve every day,

All work together, all have a say,

Not forgetting to share good seed

Giving our riches to those in need.

United we stand, Your name we own,

In You we trust, in You alone.

Now I receive all that is true, the

Everlasting love that I have in You.

Mixy shouted eloquently at Erasmus Drab, punching the air with his fist. 'You're finished Drab, no longer will you rob our citizens of their lives, allowing them to forget their purpose. Your kidology of choice is destroyed. We've remembered to put each other's needs first, to talk not ignore, and we've remembered that you are nothing in this world unless we allow you to be.' Drab dropped to the floor like a stone, paralysed by the words. They pierced His soul to the core. Defeat crossed His face.

Michael ran over to the others, and with his touch of radiance, they were restored instantly. 'But you were locked up,' stuttered Pauline, almost disbelieving her eyes.

'Erasmus Drab has skills like no other,' said Mixy. 'It seems He can mimic loved ones to fool you into thinking what He wants!'

'But where does He come from?' said Susan, looking at Drab, whose face now looked disfigured as He lay in an untidy mess, powerless on the floor. Mixy, now totally at his peak of confidence, his memory fully restored by the ancient rhyme, answered.

'We have a Great Master who gives us a free choice in life to do as we please. Things were fine in Abacus until The Master banned Erasmus Drab from the Eternal Place. Because of The Master's loving nature, He allowed Him to roam the universe. Unfortunately, He arrived here many Rivas ago, and slowly sowed the seeds of disrespect in our society. Gradually over time, things changed, but because the changes were small, no-one noticed. We all allowed things to go unchecked until eventually, everything became uncontrollable and it was easy for Him to take over. He drained the life out of us, banning The Sanguine in the whole land. It is the words of The Sanguine that remind us every day that we are loved, and that looking after each other is important.'

Mixy walked over to the wrecked character still huddled on the floor. 'There's something else I've remembered about Erasmus Drab,' and with a quick jolt, pulled at His long, curly, black hair, and off it came. Drab was completely bald, no hair on His Head, not even an eyebrow.

'I thought there was something funny about Him the first time I saw Him,' gasped Susan. 'But I just couldn't work out what it was. It was His eyebrows – well, lack of them!'

'Only beings that belong to The Master are allowed to have hair,' said Mixy. 'We are called The Redeemed.' All the children laughed with relief. Drab, who had once been likened to a handsome prince, now looked pathetic in front of the chattering crowd that had gathered in the Great Hall.

Dean asked his brother to recall what had happened after he and Kyzer had left to find Mixy. 'Well,' he began proudly, 'we went back the way we came in, didn't see Drab, thank goodness,' he said, sounding relieved. 'We ran to the other signpost at the back of the castle, where we found Mixy and Frilly. Mixy went into a frenzy when I handed him The Sanguine. He was uncontrollable for about five minutes, dancing up and down like a circus chimp.' Michael laughed. 'He attracted quite a bit of attention and soon others were jumping around like him!'

'The rest is obvious,' said Dean, giving his little brother a big squeeze. 'That's twice you've come to our rescue!' Michael beamed with delight. Those words alone were a reward in itself.

'So what's gonna happen to Drab now?' asked Pauline of Mixy.

'He's already gone,' he replied, calmly. The children gasped at his remark. Drab had somehow just disappeared in all the distraction. 'No-one can hold Him, only be held by Him. But now we know His game plan, He won't ever take Abacus again. As Mayor, I shall make sure we keep in touch with our true Master's wishes. Abacus was a wonderful place, just look at what has been forgotten. The flowers and trees have not been tended to. The ponds and lakes need clearing –it's going to take a while to make everything beautiful again.'

'Oh, I don't think so, Mixy – look!' cried Susan. 'Look, the light's breaking through the clouds, it's as if your joy is pushing up to lift them away, allowing your suns to shine properly.'

'Wow, it's getting hot,' commented Pauline. 'We only have one!' she said, screwing up her eyes slightly against the brightness.

'Up those stairs is what Drab calls his Trophy Room. It contains lots of beautiful items that we're sure don't belong in Abacus,' Dean informed Mixy.

'Don't worry, we will return them all somehow, including our new friend, Kyzer,' Mixy laughed, stroking the beautiful bird.

'I know how to get home,' he squawked excitedly, 'and Erasmus Drab bragged from where He'd got each prize, so I can help you, Mixy,' flexing his elegant wings in a clapping movement.

'Have you found your key?' Mixy asked, excitedly.

'Mission accomplished!' said Pauline and Dean, in unison, as Susan dragged the bucket over to show Mixy all the pieces.

'Crikey,' said Dean, looking down at his watch. 'The deadline! What time is it? My watch is broken!' Terror now struck the children. They had spent so much time in their conflict with Drab and then rejoicing with Mixy, that they had lost precious minutes. Would they get back in time?

'Mixy, there's so much we want to discuss with you, but there's not the time. If we don't get back, we'll be trapped here for a year,' cried Susan, as she gave Mixy a big hug.

Dean, suddenly feeling the pain of his injuries once more, said, 'we must get back right now. Have you any transport to get us to the island any quicker? I can barely walk.'

'Erasmus Drab's carriage is just outside,' said a man in a bright pink hat and rosy cheeks to match.

'Ooh, look at all the colour in you all, it's wonderful,' Pauline noticed excitedly.

The children and Mixy, carrying Dean, hurried down to Drab's carriage, passing scores of cheery people still singing The Sanguine, and waving then goodbye, like a bride and groom leaving a church. Kyzer had already flown on to the roof, his wings becoming stronger by the minute.

25

THE RACE AGAINST TIME

'Get going!' shouted Mixy at the horses, that didn't need telling a second time. As the horses sped along the sunlit path, the gang noticed everything coming to life. Pretty flowers were unfurling and lifting their heads to the welcoming sunshine. The fauna was typically tropical in Abacus due to its three suns. Now awash with colour, gigantic plants basked alongside the road, surprising onlookers with splashes of red and purple cup-like flowers. Birds flew furiously around the sky, diving at the carriage as it hurried on towards the lake, the sound of horses' hooves echoing all around.

As they approached the lake, the true beauty that had now unfolded in Abacus took them back. Everything was being restored, just as time-lapse photography would make it. Plants just bursting into blooms of fantastic colours wherever you looked. As they reached the lake, it reflected the now, clear-blue sky, reminding Susan of a posh hotel swimming pool she had seen in a travel brochure. If only there was time for a swim she thought, but time had out-run them. Precious minutes had been stolen by the encounter with Drab, and was now spoiling their last few moments in Abacus. Panic had set in at the looming deadline. Michael had left the boat hidden under bushes. Now in bright yellow, it stood out, making its discovery easy. Mixy lifted Dean into the boat.

'Oh Mixy, thank you for all your help,' said Pauline gratefully, shaking his hand.

'Yes,' said Dean, admiringly. 'You've been a star.' Mixy blushed as he had the last word.

'Your encounter in Abacus has taught us so much,' he shouted at the leaving party, as the girls began to row to the middle of the island. 'You came here to find a key – but you unlocked our hearts and minds to the truth at the same time. God bless you and take care.' The children were visibly moved at leaving Mixy, Frilly and Kyzer. They had become good companions together. They all waved frantically, with Kyzer flying overhead.

'We'll return next year Mixy, promise,' Michael shouted, tearfully. Pauline touched his shoulder to comfort the young boy, who had played such an important role in this adventure. 'I wonder who his Master is?' said Michael. 'He did say God bless.'

'Hmm, I guess we'll never find out, that's if we get back in time,' said Dean, unable to shed any light or think about anything but getting to the cave before the door closed.

'Oh God, please get us back in time,' said Susan loudly, looking up at the sky. 'I love my Mum and Dad so much, I'd really miss them, even Stinky.'

'They'll send out police searches for us all, and never find us,' shrieked Pauline, as the consequences dawned.

'Oh the worry for our Mums and Dads, they'll think we've been drowned or kidnapped for defo,' Susan pointed out, gravely. Dean and Michael tried to hide their fears, but tears began to run down Michael's cheeks as he thought about all that he was hearing, and saw the concern in the older children's faces.

Emotions were running high as the four hit the island. Would the lift be there? Susan and Pauline dragged Dean, as comfortably as they could, whilst Michael carried the key bits. Kyzer squawked a last goodbye, which was unheard by the worried children. It had been easy coming out of the cave, as the light from the entrance had guided their direction. They couldn't see a thing the other way. Now they didn't know what to follow, except their instincts. 'Which way?' said Pauline, as the darkness inside the cave hit them.

'Let's go left,' said Dean and Susan together. In a panic, Michael insisted he thought it was right, and in a desperate attempt to explore all the options before time ran out, he was off shouting Maddison's name into the air.

'Stupid kid. Supposing he gets lost,' said Susan to Dean, with her heart beating faster than ever.

'Maddison, Maddison,' shouted Pauline, not wasting any time. 'Are you there?' In a flash, green lamps lit up the lift, which was right in front of them. The doors opened and there stood Maddison with a beam on his face, then it disappeared as he realised that Michael was not with them.

'Oh Maddison, are we glad to see you!' gasped Susan. He ushered them in, carefully sitting Dean on the green operator chair. Maddison's next priority was to locate Michael.

'In one minute, the doorway to Abacus will close. Where is Michael?' he asked, urgently.

'He ran off down that passage,' they wailed. Maddison's next instructions were clear, but painful to hear.

'If I am not back by the slow count of thirty, you MUST press the second floor button.' Off he disappeared quickly, into the blackness. The longest half minute in history began, with Dean doing the counting, anxiously willing his brother to appear.

'Come on, Michael,' shouted Susan and Pauline, repeatedly in all directions from the lift entrance.

'Please make it back,' prayed Pauline, her heart nearly hitting her tonsils as the panic set in, her brow bearing tiny beads of sweat.

Suddenly, steps could be heard in the distance. The girls squealed in delight as tiny pieces of Glow Glob, still stuck to Michael's jumper, danced forward in the dark. Maddison had got him, as they both appeared out of the darkness to the count of twenty three!

'Press the button, Dean,' Maddison commanded, as he closed the metal safety gate, leaving Abacus behind. The girls grabbed hold of Michael, who was panting heavily from the run back.

'Sorry I went off,' he managed to gasp, as they let go. Then he went to bear-hug Dean, as the girls in turn were hugged by Maddison. It was a relief to see each other and spirits were high, with everyone wanting to talk at the same time. No-one felt the dull thud as the lift began to ascend to the second floor. As the doors opened to familiar surroundings, the time on Maddison's watch was exactly 9am. What a night!

26

IF ONLY

Stepping out into the hotel brought a sigh of relief to all but Susan.

'Oh heck, I've left your tape recorder in Drab's castle, what will your Dad say?' she winced.

'That's ok,' laughed Dean, just glad to be back, then punching her gently. 'We'll just have to say, *you've* lost it.'

'Remind me to keep out of his way,' she laughed. 'Here, you keep the key bits till later.'

'Shh,' whispered Maddison. 'You are all so excited, you'll get Mrs Fishwick up here. They are busy serving breakfast downstairs. I suggest you go and get some and meet back here at 11am.' That seemed a good idea under the circumstances. The excitement of the night's adventure was keeping them awake for now, but they sure were hungry! Susan and Pauline helped Dean to his room, leaving the key bits with the boys. The girls wondered whether to go back to their room or down for breakfast. Calculating that Susan's mum would have checked their room by now, they decided to head down to the dining room. The smell of eggs and bacon hurried them on. Susan spotted her family in the corner. She ran over, giving her Mum the biggest hug ever.

'Oh yes,' laughed Mrs Watson, suspiciously. 'What do you want now?'

'More money, I suspect,' said Mr Watson, not lifting his head from the morning paper.

'No, nothing at all,' said Susan, smugly. Then surprised her Dad by planting a kiss on his forehead. Pauline made a fuss of little John.

'What's got in to you two?' said Mr Watson. 'You're acting like you've never had parents.'

'Mum, Dad, sometimes you just don't appreciate what you've got and take it for granted. I'm not going to do that, ever again,' she smiled, then patted baby John on his head.

'Irene – I think she's ill,' laughed Mr Watson, putting his paper down.

'Oh yes,' interrupted Mrs Watson. 'What's with putting those teddies on your pillows to look like you're in bed – I got the fright of my life this morning!'

'Good, I'm glad you enjoyed the joke,' quipped Susan, flashing her eyes at Pauline. They sat down and ate almost double what they would normally eat, trying not to draw too much attention to themselves as Susan usually picked at her food.

'There's been a change of plan for today,' announced Mrs Watson. 'Your Grandma is coming to the hotel for her lunch.'

'What time is she arriving?' Susan quickly asked.

'About eleven thirty,' she answered. 'She's coming by taxi – I thought it would be nice if you and Pauline were to meet her at the door. We'll all go shopping later on in the afternoon for a nice treat.'

'Yeah, that'll be lovely,' she said, through an almighty yawn.

'What time did you two get to sleep?' asked Mr Watson.

'Er, I dunno,' said Susan, shaking her shoulders up and down.

'Look, Pauline's yawning now,' he said, disapprovingly. The tiredness started to race upon them. The food didn't help, you always feel more tired after a meal.

'We'll be upstairs until Grandma comes, if that's all right, Mum?' Susan said, with another wide yawn.

'Get back to bed, both of you!' said Mr Watson. 'I can see dark circles under your eyes. And change your clothes! You wore them yesterday and it looks like you've slept in them too!' he sneered.

'Alan, don't be rude, the girls said they weren't feeling very well last night,' said Mrs Watson, coming to her daughter's defence.

The girls dragged themselves up to the fourth floor, and after entering their room, flopped onto their beds. 'Set the alarm for ten thirty, P,' Susan moaned, before entering the land of nod. Pauline just managed to follow the instruction before losing consciousness. Two floors below, the boys had long entered the mysterious world of sleep.

The beeping of Pauline's alarm took its time waking up the sleepy heads.

'What, eh, turn it off someone!' mumbled Susan, in a semi-awake state. Pauline was well away in her dreams, always trying to squeeze every second of extra kip she could, except on a Saturday when she went to tap dancing lessons. She was always raring to go on this one day of the week – but not today. The tiredness hit Susan on the head like a rubber hammer. Her brain screamed out to beg extra time, but then something deep down inside seemed to know it was time to get up. 'C'mon P,' she sighed, rolling over on her back. The sun shone through a chink in the curtains, giving an eerie feel to the room.

Susan suddenly became confused. Was Abacus a dream? Where had Drab gone? She felt strange and a little panicky. She went to shake Pauline – she needed to know she wasn't crazy! 'Peewee, Peewee, wake up.' Susan shook her shoulder to gain a response.

Her eyes shot open at the jolt. 'What, what?' uttered Pauline, quickly.

'Have we been to Abacus?' said Susan, looking sternly into her friend's tired face.

'Well, I have…Mixy, Frilly and Kyzer ring any bells with you?' Pauline uttered.

'Phew, I thought I was going loopy for a few minutes,' cried Susan, letting out a deep breath.

'Let's face it,' expressed Pauline. 'If I woke up now and it HAS been a dream, I wouldn't be surprised. The whole adventure is unbelievable!' Susan sat back on her bed then noticed the bracelet on her arm.

'Ooh look,' she said, her mouth opening wide. 'Ada's bracelet.' Pauline took hold of Susan's arm to have a better look.

'Well, there's the proof. We've been to another world – weird!'

'Smart,' smiled Susan. 'C'mon, let's find Maddison and tell him what happened in Abacus.'

'Ok, but let's change our clothes first, yeah?' laughed Pauline.

The four children enjoyed telling Maddison all about their adventure, confirming it was now safe to return.

'It's a shame you can't go back for another year – I'm really sorry we didn't get back a bit earlier to allow you to return,' said Dean, disappointed.

'I've got plenty of time to go back. Don't forget, once I go back I'll live forever, so another year here will be fun.'

'I'll persuade my Mum and Dad to come here every half-term, so we can play with you,' said Susan enthusiastically.

'So will we,' Michael chipped in.

'Michael, you've not to tell a soul,' warned Dean.

'No-one will believe me anyway,' he laughed.

'How have you explained your twisted ankle and cuts, to your parents?'

'Oh, they just think I've been acting silly and had an accident. They know what I'm like. Mum's really concerned,' confessed Dean. 'The doctor's coming this afternoon to check me over.'

'You know, if it hadn't been for you, Michael, we would have been trapped there for a year, maybe forever!' said Susan, patting him on the shoulder. Michael beamed with pride and resisted showing off, just lapping up the praise.

'Twice you've saved us,' Pauline reminded him.

'Yes,' said Maddison, 'Michael was very brave, but it was your team work that won out in the end. Not one of you could have done it on your own. You can always achieve more when you work together. I remember the terrible war years before you were all born, and the way people worked together was incredible. The strength of community spirit enabled them to deal with rapid changes and restrictions, and as each played their part, they overcame the enemy. It's the lesson that Mixy has learned, remember that for the future.'

'Michael, pass us the key bits,' requested Pauline, arms outstretched, eager to start fitting all the pieces together.

'Ooh yes,' said Susan, excitedly. 'Where's your piece, Maddison?'

Dean and Pauline fumbled around for several minutes, trying to make it fit this way and that. Susan left them to it whilst she thanked Maddison for getting Michael to rescue them, and asked how he'd had the idea to send the tape recorder.

'I'd noticed how you all listened to the tunes, and how happy they made you.'

'Thank goodness it worked, but now I've met Drab, I can see how, if you allow yourself to get into something too much, you can become a slave to it without being aware. I suppose I can see now why my Dad gets so fed up of me sitting in front to the television watching programmes, night after night. While I'm doing that, I'm not talking to anyone else, getting to know them, or sharing how I feel with anyone, because I'm hooked on my favourite TV shows. In fact, I stopped going to Brownies 'cos I liked watching Coronation Street more on Wednesday nights! It will be hard, but I'm going to try and watch it a bit less and spend more time with friends.'

'Done it!' came the cry from the others. 'The piece Ada found would have fit there,' Dean informed the others, holding up the incomplete key.

'I wonder if it would work without that piece?' pondered Pauline.

'I doubt it,' said Susan. 'But perhaps another piece could be made like it?'

Maddison reminded Susan that she was meeting her Grandma at eleven thirty, and they arranged to meet again after lunch. Coming out of the broom cupboard, the girls skipped down to Reception.

<u>27</u>

<u>NO…NO, I DIDN'T SEE THAT COMING!</u>

'What are we going to do with the key now?' said Pauline. 'I mean, where do we say we found it? And hey, we'll have to split the reward, won't we?'

'Not that we mind,' laughed Susan. 'I think Michael should get it all, but don't tell him.'

'We could say we found it buried on the beach,' said Pauline. 'I always thought it might be down there before we found out where it really was.'

The sun was shining bright and a light breeze caught Grandma's hat as she stepped out of the bright blue taxi. 'C'mon Gran, grab hold of my arm, Pauline will get hold of the other,' instructed Susan, giving her a big hug at the same time.

'I hope it's something good for dinner,' said Mrs Fradd, licking her tiny lips. 'I've been dreaming of it all morning, they do such good meals here.' Suddenly, as they were entering Reception, Grandma gasped as she looked down at Susan's arm. 'My beloved bracelet,' she said, astonished. Equally taken aback were Susan and Pauline.

'Did you have one like this, Gran?' said Susan, disbelievingly.

'Yes, I dropped it years ago – did you find it here at The Seafield?' asked Mrs Fradd as she lovingly touched it on her Granddaughter's arm.

'Grandma, I think you're mistaken,' said Susan, gently. 'I didn't find it here at the hotel.'

'You know, I may be old Susie, but I'd know my bracelet anywhere. My father bought it for my tenth birthday – look inside, it's engraved A. W. for Ada Walsh, my maiden name.'

'Ada! – But your name is Alice! That's what Dad calls you!'

'Yes, your Granddad's pet name for me was Alice. He was meant to meet an Alice on a blind date and she never turned up, but he met me on the same evening, and he jokingly called me Alice all night, and that's what stuck over the years, but my real name is Ada.' Excitedly, Susan asked Pauline to help her unclasp the small bangle, and moments later all three looked at each other knowingly as the letters A. W. shone out in the sun.

'Gran – you've been to Abacus, haven't you?' said Susan, amazed that her Grandma could keep such a secret for so long.

'So you know Maddison can talk and everything, Mrs Fradd?' declared Pauline, equally astonished.

'Come on, let's get inside and I'll tell you more,' said Mrs Fradd, with great excitement in her voice at being able to unburden herself at last. The story exploded from her as they all sat down on one of the large settees in Reception, and

Grandma explained all the events from seeing Drab pinch the key to moving away to London. Bursting to talk, the girls could keep quiet no longer.

'Have you still got your piece of the key?' they asked, in suspense.

'You mean this?' said Grandma, as she reached around her small neck and pulled up the gold chain from her pink blouse. There looped on the end was a long whistle-like object. The missing piece!

'Maddison and I have been in touch ever since I returned from London when I was twenty-one. We have often talked about sending someone back. Your Mum was ill with asthma as a child, so was unable to help. But as you were growing up, I just knew that you and Pauline would have the faith and courage to have a go. So, I persuaded your Mum to come for a visit just when I knew the doorway would be open. Maddison rang me this morning and told me you had gone with young Dean and then, that you had got into trouble, and that Michael had then gone to your rescue, and of course that you were all back safely. I suggested having dinner here today to see how you had got on first-hand, and of course to bring the piece I've kept close to my heart all these years – now shush, your Dad's coming.'

'Hello Alice, are you ready for dinner?' asked Mr Watson, planting a kiss on her cheek.

'We want to claim the reward Gran, who should we tell?' whispered Susan.

'Oh yes, do you think the fountain would work after all this time?' asked Pauline, under her breath. As they made their way to the dining room, Mrs Fradd informed them that she had always kept up-to-date regarding the reward and knew who to contact about the matter, but she wanted dinner first!

Susan's Mum was most surprised after dinner when she found out her Mother wanted to go on an errand with the girls, and it was a secret. But then, her Mother had always been a little mysterious, and agreed as long as the girls didn't wear her out. Back up in Maddison's room, they all had a little party with orange juice and chocolate to celebrate the long-awaited return of the key. Dean and Michael were astonished at the fact that Susan's dear old Grandma was in fact Ada.

'Now, about the reward,' said Grandma. Everyone's eyes lit up. 'The original five pounds was invested in the stock market, and had reached quite a sizeable amount.'

'What's a stock market?' asked, you've guessed it, Susan.

Dean was in like a shot. 'Like a bank, but it's a bit risky, you can earn lots of interest, but you can also lose your money, too,' he informed her quickly, wanting to hear what Grandma had to say. She continued on.

'The stocks made a lot of money and amazingly Francis Eaves, who was guardian of the reward, sold his shares in 1928, just before the market crashed and many people lost all their money. He invested it in property.'

'My Dad says that's always a good thing to invest in,' said Dean, buzzing.

'Guess which property he invested in?' teased Grandma. Various replies were bounded across Maddison's bed, including Buckingham Palace and Blackpool Tower. None were correct. 'The Seafield Hotel, of course,' Grandma squealed with delight. Shouts were so loud that Grandma and Maddison had to calm everyone down for fear of Mrs Fishwick hearing in the kitchen below.

'Will *we* get the reward then?' asked Susan, excitedly.

'We have to contact the Treasury Department at Marlingham Town Hall, present the key and make a claim.'

'Can we do it today?' Michael asked, jumping up and down.

'The sooner the better,' agreed Grandma, rocking back and forth in her seat.

Three days had passed and the town was busy preparing for a great event. The discovery of the long lost key was in all the local newspapers plus on the world television news. The children were stars all week, giving interviews about how they had found the key in a bucket, deep down in the sand.

On the Saturday, the last day of the holidays, the present Mayor, Mr Bertram Wareing, had already arranged for the age-old vault to be opened and the key fixed in place, after oiling the cogs and pipes in preparation for the great turn-on. The fire brigade turned up to fill the fountain with gallons of water. All the bronze and silver had been polished to gleam in the summer sun, that at last had made an appearance in the town. Susan, Dean, Pauline and Michael, now joint owners of The Seafield Hotel, had asked Mr and Mrs Fishwick, who had only rented it from the Town Hall, to continue to run it in fine fashion until they were all older.

The great moment arrived. Sixty four years after it had mysteriously stopped working, it was now being turned on again, giving Marlingham a welcome return to the spotlight. The children were guests of honour and, tucking into Walnut Whips, took their places on special seats to watch the spectacular sight of cascading water come spilling down over the bronze cherubim, reading their silver books. It was indeed a wonderful sight Monsieur Lavadan had created, bringing joy especially to many older townsfolk, who had lived for all the years with its loss.

As the crowds of people gathered to enjoy the long-awaited sight, no-one noticed the handsome man dressed in black, watching at the back. 'Restoration has come temporarily to this world, He thought. But now I'm here again, it won't be long before the *poison of the ordinary* sets in amongst these humans, and then I shall be Master of this Earth for good.'

He quickly spotted a newspaper reporter in the busy line-up, and with a light touch to the man's shoulder, began to whisper in his ear.

Well, Dear Reader,

Have you noticed the effects of Erasmus Drab's work lately? After all, He's been here for some time now. Have a good think, I bet you have!

The words 'poison of the ordinary,' reprinted by permission from 'God Came Near,' by Max Lucado © 1986, Thomas Nelson Inc., Nashville, Tennessee. All rights reserved.

www.ingramcontent.com/pod-product-compliance
Lightning Source LLC
Chambersburg PA
CBHW070842120626
46556CB00002B/841